Anonymous

Laws, Regulations, Circulars, Orders, Decisions, Etc.

Anatiposi

Anonymous

Laws, Regulations, Circulars, Orders, Decisions, Etc.

Reprint of the original, first published in 1871.

1st Edition 2023 | ISBN: 978-3-38217-598-6

Anatiposi Verlag is an imprint of Outlook Verlagsgesellschaft mbH.

Verlag (Publisher): Outlook Verlag GmbH, Zeilweg 44, 60439 Frankfurt, Deutschland
Vertretungsberechtigt (Authorized to represent): E. Roepke, Zeilweg 44, 60439 Frankfurt, Deutschland
Druck (Print): Books on Demand GmbH, In de Tarpen 42, 22848 Norderstedt, Deutschland

LAWS, REGULATIONS,

CIRCULARS, ORDERS, DECISIONS, ETC.,

RELATING TO THE

U. S. NAVAL ENGINEER CORPS.

WASHINGTON:
GOVERNMENT PRINTING OFFICE.
1871.

THE UNITED STATES NAVAL ENGINEER CORPS.

ORGANIZATION, &c.

AN ACT to reorganize the Navy Department of the United States.

Be it enacted by the Senate and House of Representatives of the United States of America in Congress assembled, That there shall be established in the Navy Department the following Bureaus, to wit: Bureaus established in the Navy Department.

First. A Bureau of Yards and Docks.
Second. A Bureau of Equipment and Recruiting.
Third. A Bureau of Navigation.
Fourth. A Bureau of Ordnance.
Fifth. A Bureau of Construction and Repair.
Sixth. A Bureau of Steam Engineering.
Seventh. A Bureau of Provisions and Clothing.
Eighth. A Bureau of Medicine and Surgery.

SEC. 2. *And be it further enacted,* That the President of the United States, by and with the advice and consent of the Senate, shall appoint from the list of officers of the Navy, not below the grade of commander, a chief for each of the Bureaus of Yards and Docks, Navigation, Equipment and Recruiting, and of Ordnance, and shall in like manner appoint a chief of the Bureau of Construction and Repair, who shall be a skillful naval constructor; and shall also appoint a chief of the Bureau of Steam Engineering, who shall be a skillful engineer, and be selected from the list of chief engineers of the Navy; and shall also appoint a chief of the Bureau of Medicine and Surgery, who shall be selected from the list of the surgeons of the Navy, and a chief of the Bureau of Provisions and Clothing, who shall be selected from the list of paymasters of the Navy of not less than ten years' standing; each of which chiefs of Bureaus shall receive a salary * * * per annum,* unless otherwise heretofore provided for by law, which shall be in lieu of all other compensation whatever; the said chiefs of Bureaus to hold their said offices for the term of four years: *Provided,* That nothing herein contained shall be construed to affect any provision heretofore made by law for special cases. Chiefs of Bureaus, how appointed, and from whom to be selected.

Salaries and term of office.

SEC. 3. *And be it further enacted,* That the Secretary of the Navy shall appoint the following clerks and other officers, to wit: Clerks, &c., authorized.

* * * * * *

---

* For salary of chief of Bureau, see p. 38.

 For the Bureau of Steam Engineering, one chief clerk, at a salary of eighteen hundred dollars; one draughtsman at fourteen hundred dollars,* one clerk at fourteen hundred dollars, one assistant draughtsman at twelve hundred dollars, one messenger at eight hundred and forty dollars salary per annum, and one laborer at six hundred dollars per annum.

* * * * * *

 SEC. 4. *And be it further enacted*, That the Secretary of the Navy shall assign and distribute among the said Bureaus such of the duties of the Navy Department as he shall judge to be expedient and proper;† and all of the duties of the said Bureaus shall be performed under the authority of the Secretary of the Navy, and their orders shall be considered as emanating from him, and shall have full force and effect as such.

 SEC. 5. *And be it further enacted*, That all estimates for specific, general, and contingent expenses of the Department, and of the several Bureaus, shall be furnished to the Secretary of the Navy by the chiefs of the respective Bureaus, and all such appropriations shall be under the control and expended by the direction of the Secretary of the Navy, and the appropriation for each Bureau shall be kept separate in the Treasury.

 SEC. 6. *And be it further enacted*, That the chiefs of the respective Bureaus of the Navy Department shall be authorized to frank all communications from their respective Bureaus; and all communications to their Bureaus on the business thereof shall be free of postage. * * *

Approved July 5, 1862. (Vol. 12, p. 510.)

AN ACT in relation to franked matter.

 Be it enacted by the Senate and House of Representatives of the United States of America in Congress assembled, That all communications relating to the official business of the Department to which they are addressed, of whatever origin, addressed to the chiefs of the several Executive Departments of the Government, or to such principal officers of each Executive Department, being heads of Bureaus, or chief clerks, or one duly authorized by the Postmaster General to frank official matter, shall be received and conveyed by mail free of postage without being indorsed "official business," or with the name of the writer. ‡

Approved June 1, 1864. (Vol. 13, p. 95.)

---

* Established at $1,800 by act of March 2, 1867.

† The act of July 16, 1862, authorizes the Secretary to assign clerks and laborers attached to one Bureau, to duty in another.

‡ Among those who are authorized by the forty-second section of the act of March 3, 1863, to frank mail matter, are the chiefs of the several Executive Departments; also such principal officers, being heads of Bureaus or chief clerks, of each Executive Department, to be used only for official communications, as the Postmaster General shall by regulation prescribe.

APPOINTMENT, &c., OF ENGINEERS.

AN ACT making appropriations for the naval service for the year ending
June thirty, eighteen hundred and seventy-two, and for other purposes.

*   *   *   *   *

SEC. 10. * * * That chiefs of Bureau may be appointed
from officers having the relative rank of captain in the staff
corps of the Navy on the active list. *   *   * Appointment and title of chief of Bureau.

SEC. 12. * * * The chief of the Bureau of *   *   *
Steam Engineering shall have * the title of Engineer-in-
Chief. *   *   *

Approved March 3, 1871.

From the naval appropriation bill, approved March 3, 1845.

SEC. 7. *And be it further enacted*, That in lieu of the mode
heretofore provided by law, the Engineer-in-Chief and chief
engineers of the Navy shall be appointed by the President,
by and with the advice and consent of the Senate. * * Chief engineers to be appointed by the President.

AN ACT to amend an act entitled "An act to establish and equalize the
grade of line officers of the United States Navy," approved July sixteen,
eighteen hundred and sixty-two.

*   *   *   *   *   *

SEC. 7. *And be it further enacted*, That the President of
the United States shall appoint paymasters of the fleet and
engineers of the fleet in the same manner and with the same
rank and pay as fleet surgeons. Fleet paymasters and fleet engineers.

*   *   *   *   *   *

Approved April 21, 1864.   (Vol. 13, p. 53.)

AN ACT to regulate the appointment and pay of engineers in the Navy
of the United States.

*   *   *   *   *   *

SEC. 5. *And be it further enacted*, That the Secretary of
the Navy shall be authorized to prescribe a uniform for the
said chief engineers and assistant engineers, and to make
all necessary rules and regulations for the proper arrangement and government of the Corps of Engineers and assistant engineers, not inconsistent with the Constitution and
laws of the United States. The said engineers and assistant engineers shall be, in all respects, subject to the laws,
rules, and regulations of the naval service, in like manner
with other officers of the service. Uniform for engineers and rules for their government to be prescribed.
Engineers subject to laws and regulations of the Navy.

*   *   *   *   *   *

Approved August 31, 1842.. (Vol. 5, p. 577.)

AN ACT to define the number and regulate the appointment of officers
in the Navy, and for other purposes.

*   *   *   *   *   *

SEC. 7. *And be it further enacted*, That naval constructors
and first and second assistant engineers in the Navy shall
be appointed by the President and confirmed by the Senate,
and shall have naval rank and pay as officers of the Navy. Assistant engineers to be appointed by the President.

*   *   *   *   *   *

Approved July 25, 1866.

REGULATIONS FOR THE APPOINTMENT OF CADET ENGINEERS.

I. In pursuance of the third and fourth sections of an act passed at the first session of the Thirty-eighth Congress, approved July 4, 1864, "*To authorize the Secretary of the Navy to provide for the education of naval constructors and engineers, and for other purposes*," and of the second section of an act passed at the first session of the Thirty-ninth Congress, approved March 2, 1867, entitled "*An act to amend certain acts in relation to the Navy*," applications will be received ·by the Navy Department for the appointment of cadet engineers.

II. The application is to be addressed to the Secretary of the Navy, and can be made by the candidate, or by any person for him, and his name will be placed on the register. The registry of a name, however, gives no assurance of an appointment, and no preference will be given in the selection to priority of application.

III. The number of cadet engineers is limited by law to fifty. The candidate must be not less than eighteen nor more than twenty-two years of age; he will be required to certify *on honor* to his precise age, to the Academic Board, previous to his examination, and no one will be examined who is over or under the prescribed age. His application must be accompanied by satisfactory evidence of moral character and health, with information regarding date of birth and educational advantages hitherto enjoyed. Candidates who receive permission will present themselves to the Superintendent of the Naval Academy, between the 15th and 25th of September, for examination as to their qualifications for admission.

IV. The course of study will comprise two academic years. All cadets who graduate will be warranted as assistant engineers in the Navy. The pay of a cadet engineer is the same as that of a cadet midshipman.

V. The academic examinations previous to appointment will be on the following subjects, namely: *Arithmetic;* the candidate will be examined in numeration and the addition, subtraction, multiplication, and division of whole numbers and of vulgar and decimal fractions; in reduction; in proportion, or rule of three, direct and inverse; extraction of square and cube roots; in *Algebra*, (Bourdon's,) through equations of the first degree; in *Geometry*, (Davies's Legendre,) through the plane figures; *Rudimentary Natural Philosophy; Reading;* he must read clearly and intelligibly from any English narrative work; as, for example, Bancroft's History of the United States; in *Writing* and *Spelling;* he must write from dictation, in a legible hand, and spell with correctness, both orally and in writing; in *English Grammar* and *English Composition;* he will be examined as to the parts of speech, the rules connected therewith, and the elementary construction of sentences, and will be required to write such original paragraphs as will show that he has a proper knowledge of the subject. The candidate will also be required to exhibit a fair degree of proficiency in pencil-sketching, and to produce satisfactory evidence of mechanical aptitude. Candidates who possess greatest skill and experience in the practical knowledge of machinery, other qualifications being equal, shall have precedence for admission.

VI. Any of the following conditions will be sufficient to reject a candidate:

Feeble constitution, permanently impaired general health, decided cachexia, all chronic diseases or results of injuries that would permanently impair efficiency, viz:

1. Infectious disorders.
2. Weak or disordered intellect.
3. Unnatural curvature of spine.
4. Epilepsy, or other convulsion, within five years.
5. Chronic impaired vision, or chronic disease of the organs of vision.
6. Great permanent hardness of hearing, or chronic disease of the ears.
7. Loss or decay of teeth to such an extent as to interfere with digestion and impair health.
8. Impediment of speech to such an extent as to impair efficiency in the performance of duty.
9. Decided indications of liability to pulmonary disease.
10. Permanent inefficiency of either of the extremities.
11. Hernia.
12. Incurable sarcocele, hydrocele, fistula, stricture, or hæmorrhoids.
13. Large varicose veins of lower limbs.   Chronic ulcers.
14. Attention will also be paid to the stature of the candidate, and no one *manifestly* undersized for his age will be received into the Academy. In case of doubt about the physical condition of the candidate, any marked deviation from the usual standard of height will add materially to the consideration for rejection.
15. The board will exercise a proper discretion in the application of the above conditions to each case, rejecting no candidate who is likely to be efficient in the service, and admitting no one who is likely to prove physically inefficient.

VII. If both these examinations result favorably, the candidate will receive an appointment as a cadet engineer, become an inmate of the Academy, and will be allowed his actual and necessary traveling expenses from his residence to the Naval Academy, and be required to sign articles by which he will bind himself to serve in the United States Navy six years, (including his term of probation at the Naval Academy,) unless sooner discharged; if, on the contrary, he shall not pass both of these examinations, he will receive neither an appointment nor his traveling expenses, nor can he have the privilege of another examination for admission *to the same class*, unless recommended by the board of examiners.

VIII. When candidates shall have passed the required examinations, and been admitted as members of the Academy, they must immediately furnish themselves with the following articles, viz:

One Navy-blue uniform suit,	One pair of blankets,
One fatigue suit,	One bed cover or spread,
One Navy-blue uniform cap,	Two pairs of sheets,
One uniform overcoat,	Four pillow-cases,
Ten pairs of white pants,	Six towels,
Four white vests,	Two pairs of shoes or boots,
Six white shirts,	One hair-brush,
Six pairs of socks,	One tooth-brush,
Four pairs of drawers,	One clothes-brush,
Six pocket-handkerchiefs,	One coarse comb for the hair,
One black-silk handkerchief or stock,	One fine comb for the hair,
One mattress,	One tumbler or mug, and
One pillow,	One thread and needle case.

Room-mates will jointly procure, for their common use, one looking-glass, one wash-basin, one water-pail, one slop-bucket, and one broom. These articles may be obtained from the storekeeper of the Academy, of good quality and at fair prices.

IX. Each cadet engineer must, on admission, deposit with the paymaster the sum of seventy-five dollars, for which he will be credited on the books of that officer, to be expended by direction of the Superintendent for the purchase of text-books and other authorized articles besides those enumerated in the preceding article.

X. While at the Academy the cadets will be examined, from time to time, according to the regulations prescribed by the Navy Department; and if found deficient at any examination, or dismissed for misconduct, they cannot, by law, be continued in the Academy or naval service, except upon recommendation of the academic board.

XI. A cadet engineer who voluntarily resigns his appointment will be required to refund the amount paid him for traveling expenses.

GEO. M. ROBESON,
Secretary of the Navy.

Navy Department, April 4, 1871.

REGULATIONS FOR ADMISSION AND PROMOTION IN THE ENGINEER CORPS OF THE NAVY.

Before persons can be appointed assistant engineers in the Navy they must have passed an examination by naval surgeons as to their physical fitness, and a satisfactory examination before a board designated by the Secretary of the Navy, as the wants of the service require.

Application for permission to appear before such board must be made in writing to the Secretary of the Navy, stating the age and residence of the applicant, and must be accompanied by satisfactory testimonials as to good moral character, correct habits, and sound constitution. The application will be registered, and when the board next meets permission will be sent to the applicant, at the discretion of the Department, stating the time and place of the meeting of the board.

A candidate for an appointment to the grade of second assistant engineer must be not less than nineteen, nor more than twenty-six years of age; he must have been employed in drawing and the fabrication of machinery for not less than eighteen months in a steam-engine manufactory, or else have served not less than that period as an engineer or assistant engineer on board a steamer provided with a condensing engine; and must have obtained certificates from the director or superintending engineer as to his abilities, or else have been a graduate of the Naval Academy. The candidate must read clearly, correctly, and intelligently; he must write from dictation in a fair, legible hand, spelling and punctuating correctly, and will be required to compose an original paragraph. In arithmetic, he will be examined in numeration, and the addition, subtraction, multiplication, and division of whole numbers, and of vulgar and decimal fractions; in reduction, the rule of three, direct and inverse; and also in the mensuration of surfaces and solids of the regular forms. In steam machinery he will be required to sketch or describe the important parts of ordinary condensing and non-condensing engines; to explain their uses and mechanical operation; to explain the manner of putting engines in operation; how to regulate and modify their action; and the manner of guarding against danger from the boilers, due to foaming or other causes, by the means usually applied to them for that purpose.

Candidates for promotion to the grade of first assistant engineer must have served at least three years at sea as second assistant engineer on board a naval steamer; favorable testimonials must have been received by the Department concerning them, from the commanding officers and senior engineers under whom they may have served. They must also pass, before the board appointed to examine them, a thorough examination upon the subjects prescribed for second assistant engineers; and, in addition thereto, be able to explain properly the principles, peculiarities, and uses of the different kinds of valves and valve-gear applied to marine steam machinery; the construction, principles, peculiarities, and uses of the various apparatus for working steam expansively; the construction of the various marine boilers commonly used, together with their attachments, the uses of the same, and the reasons therefor; the modes in use of preserving boilers from decay, and of keeping steam machinery in repair; the causes of derangement in the operation of air and feed pumps and their appurtenances, and how to prevent and remedy them; the chemistry of boiler scale, the means of preventing it, and the mode of removing it; the construction, principles, peculiarities, and uses of the different kinds of surface condensers; how to calculate the loss by blowing off, with the sea water in the boiler, at a given concentration; the principles of, the manner of using, and the method of graduating the various instruments for determining the concentration of the water; the theory of using steam expansively, together with the limits and modifications imposed by practice, and the necessary calculations connected therewith; the construction and mode of applying the indicator, and the interpretation of its diagrams; the construction and principles of the various steam and vacuum gauges, and the causes of their derangement; and, besides, they must have a thorough knowledge of rudimentary mechanics; be well versed in the elements of geometry, descriptive geometry, and plane trigonometry; and be well acquainted with the practical building and repairing of steam machinery.

Candidates for promotion to the grade of chief engineer must have served at least two years at sea as first assistant engineer on board a naval steamer; favorable testimonials concerning them must have been received by the Department from the commanding officers and senior engineers under whom they may have served. They must also pass, before the board appointed to examine them, a thorough examination upon the subjects prescribed for first assistant engineers, and, in addition thereto, they must satisfy it that they are well versed in mechanical philosophy; the physical laws of steam; applied mechanics; the theory of the steam-engine; and likewise in the construction, principles, and laws of action of various types of marine governors; paddle-wheels and screw-propellers; and in all the necessary calculations relating to them. Furthermore, they must satisfy the board that they are thoroughly acquainted with the various kinds of paddle-wheel and screw-propeller engines, and must be able to point out their respective advantages and disadvantages, to design and erect the same, and to proportion them to a given vessel for a given speed, with a given propelling instrument; that they are thoroughly versed in the strength of materials, in the theoretical laws governing form, the limits and modifications imposed by practice, and the reasons connected therewith; that they are familiar with the different kinds of boilers, their respective advantages and disadvantages, and able properly to proportion and construct the same for supplying a given power under given conditions; they must be able to furnish working drawings of different kinds of engines, boilers, screw-propellers and water-wheels in use; to superintend their construction, determine upon their accuracy and fitness for use, and decide upon the different kinds of materials and metals entering into the construction of machinery; they will also satisfy the board of their sufficient knowledge of so much of chemistry as is involved in the laws of combustion; corrosion, and the metallurgic operations connected with steam-engineering.

Candidates for promotion who may fail to pass a satisfactory examination shall be examined again, once, upon the expiration of at least one year; and if they fail to pass at the second examination, they shall be dropped from the list of engineers.

Candidates for admission or promotion will be required to furnish the board of examiners with evidence of their abilities in the execution of mechanical drawings, and of their proficiency in penmanship.

The examining boards will report the relative qualifications of the persons examined, and number them, giving to the best qualified the lowest number.

When other qualifications are equal, candidates whose skill and abilities are superior in the practical knowledge of the fabrication and repair of machinery will have precedence over others for admission or promotion, who may be considered equal in other particulars.

GEO. M. ROBESON,
Secretary of the Navy.

NAVY DEPARTMENT,
    Washington, December 12, 1870.

FORM OF APPLICATION.

————, ———— —, 187–.

SIR: I respectfully make application for examination as to my qualifications for appointment as second assistant engineer in the United States Navy. I certify on honor that I was — years of age on the — day of ————, 187–, and reside in ————, in the county of ———— and State of ————. I forward herewith testimonials of moral and physical qualifications.

    Very respectfully,

———— ————.

Hon. ———— ————,
    Secretary of the Navy, Washington, D. C.

FORM OF REPORT TO BE MADE BY THE BOARD OF EXAMINERS.

NAVY-YARD, ————,
———— —, 187–.

SIR: In obedience to your order of ———— —, we have thoroughly and carefully examined ———— ———— on the subject prescribed in the Regulations for admission and promotion in the Engineer Corps of the Navy, under date of December 12, 1870, and have the honor to report, that he is professionally qualified to perform all the duties of a ———— engineer, and he has produced satisfactory evidence of his moral character and fitness for an officer of the Navy, and we recommend him to be commissioned as a ———— engineer from ————, with ranking number.

    The certificate of the examining surgeon is hereto annexed.

    Very respectfully, your obedient servants,

———— ————.
———— ————.
———— ————.

———— ————,
    Secretary of the Navy.

ENLISTMEMT, ETC., OF MEN.

No machinists, firemen, or coal-heavers shall be shipped as such until they have passed a satisfactory examination by one or more medical officers of the Navy in respect to their health and vigor, nor shall machinists or firemen be so shipped until they have passed a satisfactory examination by one or more engineer officers of the Navy upon their ability to manage fires properly with different kinds of fuel, and to use skillfully smith's tools in the repair and preservation of steam machinery and boilers. *(Firemen and coal-heavers to be examined by surgeons. And by engineer.)*

*   *   *   *   *   *

Should any machinist, fireman, or coal-heaver be reported by the senior engineer of the vessel for neglect of his duty, or inability to perform it, from other causes than sickness, or injury received in line of duty, the commanding officer of the squadron, or in his absence the commanding officer of the vessel to which such machinist, fireman, or coal-heaver belongs, may, if he deems it necessary, direct another person to perform it during the continuance of such neglect or disability, or until the place is supplied by a person of the proper rating, and the person so appointed shall receive the pay of the situation which he may thus fill. But the commanding officer shall, when it is practicable, direct first-class firemen to supply the places of machinists; second-class firemen to succeed or supply the places of the first class; and the coal-heavers, if qualified, should take the place of the second-class firemen in preference to other persons. *(In case of neglect of duty, his place to be supplied.)*

*   *   *   *   *   *

Machinists, firemen, and coal-heavers, when unable to perform their duties from other causes than sickness, or injury received in line of duty, or when they neglect them, shall receive only a reduced pay; that is, machinists shall have one-tenth deducted from their pay; firemen of the first class shall only receive the pay of firemen of the second; those of the second, the pay of coal-heavers; and coal-heavers the pay of ordinary seamen, so long as they neglect their duties or are unable to perform them, or until discharged from the service. *(Pay to be reduced in case of inability or neglect.)*

QUALIFICATIONS FOR PETTY OFFICERS IN THE ENGINEER DEPARTMENT OF A NAVAL VESSEL.

I. A candidate for the position of machinist, boiler-maker, or coppersmith must be not less than twenty, nor more than forty years old. He must pass an examination in presence of the commanding officer of the rendezvous, by at least one naval engineer, as to his qualifications as a machinist, boiler-maker, or coppersmith, and must also undergo the usual medical examination touching his physical fitness for the naval service.

II. He must also be able to read, and to write with sufficient correctness to keep the steam-log of his watch. He must know the names and uses of the various parts of a marine engine, understand the uses and management of the various ganges, cocks, and valves, how to raise steam, start a marine engine, regulate its action, and stop it.

He must know how to ascertain the height and density of the water in the boilers, how to check foaming, and guard against other danger from the boilers, how and when to regulate the quantity of the injection water, to guard against danger from water in the cylinders, and the measures to be taken in the event of a journal becoming heated, and, in short, how to act on the occurrence of any of the ordinary casualties of the engine-room.

III. The monthly pay of a machinist will be $55; of a boiler maker, $40; and of a coppersmith, $40; besides the usual ration.

IV. On first-rate ships there will be allowed three machinists, one boiler-maker, and one coppersmith; and on the second and third rates, two machinists, one boiler-maker, and one coppersmith.

WM. REYNOLDS,
Chief of Bureau of Equipment and Recruiting.

AN ACT to prescribe an oath of office, and for other purposes.

Oath of office for persons in the military, naval, and civil service.

Be it enacted by the Senate and House of Representatives of the United States of America in Congress assembled, That hereafter every person elected or appointed to any office of honor or profit under the Government of the United States, either in the civil, military, or naval departments of the public service, excepting the President of the United States, shall, before entering upon the duties of such office, and before being entitled to any of the salary or other emoluments thereof, take and subscribe the following oath or affirmation: "I, A B, do solemnly swear (or affirm) that I have never voluntarily borne arms against the United States since I have been a citizen thereof; that I have voluntarily given no aid, countenance, counsel, or encouragement to persons engaged in armed hostility thereto; that I have neither sought nor accepted nor attempted to exercise the functions of any office whatever under any authority or pretended authority in hostility to the United States; that I have not yielded a voluntary support to any pretended government, authority, power, or constitution within the United States, hostile or inimical thereto. And I do further swear (or affirm) that, to the best of my knowledge and ability, I will support and defend the Constitution of the United States against all enemies, foreign and domestic; that I will bear true faith and allegiance to the same; that I take this obligation freely, without any mental reservation or purpose of evasion; and that I will well and faithfully discharge the duties of the office on which I am about to enter: so help me God."

Oath to be preserved.

Which said oath, so taken and signed, shall be preserved among the files of the court, House of Congress, or department to which the said office may appertain. And any person who shall falsely take the said oath shall be guilty of perjury, and on conviction, in addition to the penalties now prescribed for that offense, shall be deprived of his office and rendered incapable forever after of holding any office or place under the United States.

False oath perjury.

Penalty.

Approved July 2, 1862. (Vol. 12, p. 502.)

AN ACT repealing certain provisions of law concerning seamen on board public and private vessels of the United States.

* * * * * *

Officers of vessels of the United States shall in all cases be citizens of the United States.

Approved June 28, 1864.   (Vol. 13, p. 201.)

AN ACT to increase and regulate the pay of the Navy of the United States.

* * * * * *

SEC. 3. *And be it further enacted*, That hereafter no service shall be regarded as sea-service but such as shall be performed at sea under the orders of a Department, and in vessels employed by authority of law.

* * * * * *

Approved June 1, 1860.   (Vol. 12, p. 23.)

AN ACT making appropriations for the naval service for the year ending June thirty, eighteen hundred and seventy-two, and for other purposes.

* * * * * *

Any staff officer of the Navy who has performed the duty of chief of a Bureau of the Navy Department for a full term shall thereafter be exempt from sea-duty, except in time of war.

* * * * * *

Approved March 3, 1871.

AN ACT to amend certain acts in relation to the Navy.

* * * * * *

SEC. 9. *And be it further enacted*, That officers on the retired and reserved lists of the Navy shall be entitled to promotion as their several dates upon the active list are promoted; but such promotion shall not entitle them to any pay beyond that to which they were entitled when retired, unless upon active duty, when they shall receive the full pay of their respective grades.

* * * * * *

Approved March 2, 1867.

AN ACT making appropriations for the naval service for the year ending June thirtieth, eighteen hundred and seventy-one, and for other purposes.

* * * * * *

SEC. 7. If an officer of a class subject to examination before promotion shall be absent on duty, and by reason of such absence, or of other cause not involving fault on his part, shall not be examined at the time required by law or regulation, and shall afterward be examined and found qualified, the increased rate of pay to which his promotion would entitle him shall commence from the date when he would have been entitled to it had he been examined and found qualified at the time so required by law or regulation; and this rule shall apply to any cases of this description which may have heretofore occurred. And in every such case the period of service of the party, in the grade to which he was promoted, shall, in reference to the rate of his pay, be considered to have commenced from the date when he was so entitled to take rank.

Officers to be dropped after failure upon re-examination.
SEC. 8. *And be it further enacted*, That any officer of the Navy on the active list below the grade of commander, who, upon examination for promotion, shall not be found professionally qualified, shall be suspended from promotion for one year, with corresponding loss of date, when he shall be re-examined, and in case of his failure upon such re-examination, he shall be dropped from the service.

*　　*　　*　　*　　*　　*

Approved July 15, 1870.

DUTIES, &c.

[Extracts from naval laws, 1865.—General duties, &c.]

FLEET ENGINEER.

When a chief engineer is detailed to discharge the duties of fleet engineer he will be attached to the flag-ship. His duties will be as follows, under the orders of the commander-in-chief:

1st. To exercise a general supervision over all the engineers of the fleet or squadron.

2d. To acquaint himself with the different kinds of engines in use in the squadron, and to take care that all means are used to keep them in the highest state of efficiency.

3d. To make, under the orders of the commander-in-chief, frequent inspections of the machinery, and to decide upon all ordinary repairs.

4th. To recommend surveys when the imperfections or accidents are serious, and to make reports where carelessness is suspected.

5th. To see that every vessel is provided with the necessary tools, stores, and spare parts of machinery, and that every engine and boiler is cared for properly.

6th. To examine the coal used and report to the commander-in-chief if there is any falling off in quality, or any undue dampness liable to produce spontaneous combustion.

7th. To see that the coal is properly stored at the different depots, and that there is at all times a sufficient quantity on hand to meet the probable wants of the squadron.

8th. To make frequent reports to the commander-in chief of the condition of the engineer's department of every vessel in the squadron.

9th. To examine all returns and requisitions made by the fleet or squadron, and to forward them promptly, with such remarks as he may deem necessary.

10th. To recommend to the commander-in-chief such measures as will, in his opinion, promote efficiency, economy, and uniformity in his department of the service.

11th. And finally, to perform such duties relating to his position as shall be assigned to him by the commander-in-chief.

CHIEF ENGINEER.

A chief engineer, on being ordered to a ship, will make himself acquainted with all parts of the machinery and boilers, the coal-bunkers and store-rooms; he will examine carefully all parts of the machinery and everything pertaining to it, and report to the commanding officer anything that is defective.

He will cause the assistant engineers, on their joining the vessel, to become familiar with all the cocks, valves, pipes, and the different parts of the machinery and boilers.

He will see that he has the requisite amount of stores of good quality on board, and that they are stowed away in good condition.

He will provide a supply of oatmeal to be issued to the firemen and coal-heavers without charge, at such time and in such quantities as the commanding officer may direct.

He will keep a strict account of, and be responsible for, the expenditure of the coals, stores, duplicate pieces, and all articles in the engineer department; he will examine each day's expenditure and approve it by his signature.

He will make out the watch, quarter, fire, and cleaning bills for the engineer department, assigning to each person his proper station and duty, and submit the same to the commander of the vessel for his approval and signature, which bills shall then be hung up in some conspicuous place where all persons in the department may refer to them. He will see that the prescribed duties are performed in a proper manner, and will report all neglect of duty or other breach of discipline in the fire or engine-room to the executive officer.

He will see that the fires are never lighted, nor hauled after being lighted, without the consent of the commanding officer, and that the engines are never turned after being stopped, except in obedience to signal, or by permission of the officer of the deck.

He will report to the commander any accident or defect that may occur to the machinery, boilers, and their dependencies, and at meridian of each day report the quantity of coals consumed, the revolutions made by the engines, and the average revolutions per minute for the last twenty-four hours, also the quantity of coal remaining on hand; and if at any time, in his judgment, the machinery is driven too hard, or undue strain put upon any of its parts by stress of weather, motion, or position of the vessel, he will report the same to the commander, noting such report and the causes for it in the steam-log.

He shall, make a daily personal inspection of all parts of the vessel occupied by the engines and their dependencies, and will report them ready for inspection to the executive officer at such times as may be directed by the commander of the vessel.

He shall at the setting of the watch in the evening, report the condition of the engines, boilers, and their dependencies, to the commanding officer.

He will exercise a vigilant supervision over every part of the steam department, and see that it is kept in good order; he will be particular that the steam-pumps, hose, and other means for extinguishing fires are ready for immediate use; that the water in the boilers is not carried to an improper density, and that the coals and stores are used to the greatest advantage.

He shall afford every facility and encourage in every way the assistant engineers to improve themselves in their profession.

He will examine the bunkers each time the ship arrives in port, or oftener, to see if the amount of coals correspond with the log, and if any discrepancy appears, he will report the same immediately to the commanding officer and note it on the log.

He will, on the discontinuance of steaming, with the permission of the commanding officer, clean and repair at once the engines and their dependencies.

He will cause the firemen to be instructed so as to qualify them for managing the engines and dependencies with safety, in case accident or other causes should prevent the attendance of the engineer.

He will cause the temperature of the coal-bunkers to be ascertained twice in each watch, and have the result reported to the officer of the deck.

Whenever a distilling-apparatus is fitted on board a steamship, he is to take charge of it, and will be held responsible for its being kept in proper repair and condition.

A steam-log is always to be kept when the vessel is moved by steam, which log is to be signed in the column of remarks by the engineers of the respective watches at the expiration of their watch, and at noon of each day by the senior engineer of the vessel. The steam log-book is to be handed to the commander of the vessel daily. At the end of each quarter he shall send to the commanding officer of the vessel a fair copy of the steam log book, certified by his own signature.

He will take the utmost care in the arrangement of stores, the use of lights and fires, and the adoption of every precautionary measure to prevent the danger from fire to which steamers are so much exposed.

He will carefully note in the steam-log the draught of water of the vessel and immersion of the bucket-boards just before going to sea and on arriving in port, and frequently when receiving coal or other stores.

The chief engineer will make a quarterly report, to accompany the quarterly synopsis of the steam-log, in which he will detail the breakage or other casualties of the machinery, the causes thereof as far as he may be able to ascertain with certainty, the time expended in repairing them and adjusting the machinery, and whether done by his department on board or by workmen from the shore.

He will also give his opinion of the present condition of the machinery, mentioning particularly the cylinders and their valves, the main journals, the connecting-rod journals, the steam-bearings, the pumps, the condensers and boilers, and the paddle-wheels or screw, to which he will add his observations as to their sufficiency and efficiency. In the event of any experimental machinery being on board, or unusual arrangement, he will particularly describe it and its mode of action, and give the results therefrom and his opinion on its merits. He will state the maximum speed of the vessel under steam alone, in smooth water, that can be sustained for twelve consecutive hours with the machinery in its existing condition, and give the necessary data in connection therewith, such as the boiler pressure, the number of revolutions of the engines per minute, vacuum in the condenser, number of holes of throttle-valve open, point of cutting off steam, temperatures, pounds of coal consumed per hour, number of tons of coal on board the vessel, indicated horse-power, &c. He will state the number of engineers, of first and second class firemen and coal-heavers attached to the vessel, and also the number of tons of coal that the bunkers will contain. He will add such observations on the machinery and vessel as his experience may suggest, with a view to their correct appreciation and value. A copy of the tabular synopsis and of the report is to be pasted into each quarterly steam-log, and another is to be forwarded through the prescribed channels to the Department.

ASSISTANT ENGINEERS.

When there is no chief engineer on board, the duties assigned to him will devolve on the senior assistant engineer.

Assistant engineers are at all times faithfully and zealously to carry into prompt execution all orders they may receive from the engineer officer in charge on board, or others their superiors; and they are to be especially careful in the management of the engines, boilers, and their dependencies; to adhere strictly to the directions of the engineer in charge, and to report to him instantly on discovering anything going wrong about them.

When the engines are in operation, the engineer of the watch will execute promptly all orders he may receive from the officer of the deck, though he must be careful in so doing that no risk of injury is incurred.

He will make hourly reports to the officer of the deck whether the engines and their dependencies, the force-pumps, hose, and all other means for extinguishing fire, are in good order, and that the pumps and hose are ready for immediate use. Should anything occur to require a change in the orders under which the engineer is then acting, or should special attention be required to any object in order to insure safety or more efficiency, he will report the same to the officer of the deck immediately.

Should it be necessary, from any cause, to stop the engines suddenly, he will report the fact to the officer of the deck; if not possible to do so in time before stopping them, he will report afterward his reasons therefor, and the probable length of time they will be stopped. He will also inform the chief engineer immediately.

He will note hourly on the steam-log all the information which the columns in it require, and place in the column of " remarks" full information of the state of the weather and sea, and all accidents to or defects in the engines or their dependencies, the manner of their working, the quality of the coal, and any other circumstance which may be useful for determining the powers and qualities of the vessel and the engines, under the various circumstances to which they may be exposed.

He will be particularly careful to prevent the waste of coals, oil, tallow, and all other stores in the engineer's department.

In the absence of the senior engineer officer belonging to the vessel, the one remaining on board highest in rank or seniority is to be held responsible for the good order of the engine-room, and for the proper discharge of all the duties connected therewith.

CHIEF ENGINEER OF A NAVY-YARD.

When a chief engineer of the Navy shall be attached to a navy-yard he shall, under the direction of the commandant, have the superintendence of the construction and repairs of the steam and other machinery.

He shall have the supervision, under the commandant, of the foremen and other men employed in the machine and boiler shops and foundries,

2 E C

and of all the material used in those departments, and be responsible for its preservation and proper use.

He will carefully examine, weigh, or measure all articles, whether received on contracts or open purchases, and only give receipts for them after they have been found to agree with the terms of the contract or advertisement, and, if so, enter them immediately on his books, and make out the bills without delay, certify them, and hand them to the commandant for approval, to be transmitted to the parties in interest.

All requisitions for materials or articles in his department are to be made by the foremen employed under his direction, and, when countersigned by him, are to be submitted for the approval of the commandant of the yard, who will allow such as he may deem necessary. No articles or materials are to be purchased without previous requisitions, nor are any to be used till they are duly inspected, approved, and received. He will have proper requisitions made to cover the expenditure of all articles or materials which may have been used or condemned during the preceding half month by the master-workmen.

He will have made out and sign the semi-monthly and other reports in his department that are required to be made by the commandant of the yard to the Bureau of Steam Engineering, the commandant causing him to be furnished with the costs and expenditures necessary for this purpose.

Foremen under him will report, at the middle and end of each month, the expenditure of materials and labor upon the several objects under their immediate superintendence.

He will have an exact account kept of all materials and labor expended on each and every object, and report to the commandant semi-monthly the operations on the same, distinguishing the number and classes of men employed, and the kind and quantities of materials used in each.

He will prepare duplicate pay-rolls in his office for paying the men, the original of which is to be sent to the commandant of the yard, in due time for his approval, and transmitted to the paymaster of the yard, and the duplicate forwarded to the Bureau. These pay-rolls must be certified by him.

He will supply all vessels fitting for sea with the articles to be issued from his department, taking receipts for the same, and transmitting them to the Bureau.

He will not deliver or issue any article out of the store without taking a proper receipt at the time of delivery, and, when a vessel has been fully equipped and fitted for her cruise, he will make an inventory, in duplicate, of all articles, with their cost, furnished the vessel, one of which is to be delivered to the chief engineer of the vessel before sailing, signed by himself, and the other forwarded to the Bureau, receipted by the chief engineer of the vessel.

When stores have been landed, surveyed, and disposed of, he will furnish the Bureau with a statement, showing the total value of them, in order that the vessel may be credited with the amount. All stores so landed from vessels must be kept separately.

He shall attend all sales and surveys of articles under the cognizance of the Bureau of Steam Engineering.

Such stores as are condemned he will take care are disposed of as the survey, approved by the Bureau, directs, but in no case is he to allow articles to be sacrificed through sales at auction.

He will be careful to make timely requisitions upon the Bureau for all articles which he is expected to have in charge, in order to answer promptly the demands that may be made upon him, and he will be held responsible for all deficiencies.

He will, at the end of each fiscal year, submit to the commandant a report of the engines and boilers that have been made or repaired, showing the original estimate and the actual expenditure.

The chief engineer of the yard will have the work done as required by the inspector of machinery afloat, after approval by the commandant. (See Section 18—*Officers in charge of stores.*)

CHIEF ENGINEERS APPOINTED AS INSPECTORS OF MACHINERY AFLOAT.

The inspector of steam machinery afloat is to have charge of all steam machinery afloat, at the yard or station, under the direction of the commandant, whether the vessel be under repairs or in ordinary; and he is to exercise control over all employés in the engineer's department on board such vessel.

He is held responsible for the condition and preservation of all the machinery of the vessels under his charge. When a steamer is to be laid up at the yard, he will take charge of the machinery at the time the chief engineer of the vessel is detached, and when repairs are to be effected he will make requisition on the commandant for the work necessary.

The inspector of machinery will make monthly reports to the commandant of the condition of the engineer's department of all vessels under his charge, mentioning all repairs required, and will use all proper means for the preservation of their engines, boilers, and appurtenances.

He will strictly conform to all the orders he may receive from the commandant of the yard, in relation to repair and preservation of machinery, boilers, tools, &c., of the vessels under his charge.

OFFICERS COMMANDING STEAM-VESSELS.

When an officer shall be appointed to the command of a steam-vessel, he is to observe carefully the following directions, in addition to those prescribed in the next section, relating to "officers commanding vessels:"

He is to use all possible diligence to make himself acquainted with the principles and construction of the engines, the intention and effect of the various parts of the machinery, the time the engines were constructed, the repairs they may have undergone, the period when the last repairs were made, and when the vessel last received new boilers.

As a material saving in the consumption of fuel may be produced by reducing the engine power, without reducing essentially the speed, and as occasions for this exercise of economy may frequently occur, he is to make himself acquainted with the principle and effect of the expansion of steam, and to require that the expansion gear should at all times be brought into play when the engines are not worked up to their full power.

In order to ascertain the capabilities of the ship under his command, he is, as soon as he proceeds to sea, to make careful and repeated trials by using the steam expansively, under every variety of wind and weather, draught of water, and other circumstances, so as to be able at all times to apply the principle of expansion, according to the nature of the service on which he may be engaged, and to calculate with accuracy the number of days the ship can be under steam without being obliged to put into port for fuel.

Vessels under steam will never use more than two-thirds of their boiler-power unless in an emergency, which must be fully entered and explained upon the log, and a special report of the same made to the Bureau of Steam Engineering.

When paddle-wheel steamers are running long distances in the trades, with the wind free, the paddles in the water are to be removed and the vessel navigated under sail alone. Under other circumstances, steam may be used according to the foregoing paragraph.

As to the use of sails, either with or without the use of steam, or as to moderating the steam when running head to wind and sea, each commanding officer must be guided by his own judgment, but with the understanding that he must be prepared to justify every expenditure of fuel for steaming purposes if called upon to do so. His judgment will necessarily be based upon a consideration of the urgency and nature of the service to be performed, of the wind and weather, and upon the difficulties of the navigation and the qualities of the vessel; but he is to take care, first, that steam is not used at all when the service can be equally or nearly as well performed without it; secondly, that sail is never dispensed with when it can be employed to advantage to assist the steam; and thirdly, that full steam power is never employed unless in chase, or absolutely necessary, the cause for which must be reported to the Department in writing.

He is carefully to inform himself of the usual daily consumption of coal, and to obtain all information in regard to the most economical and efficient use of the engines and their appendages.

To prevent accidents by spontaneous combustion, he is to order the greatest care to be observed that the coal is not taken aboard when wet, and that when on board it is kept as dry as possible. When a fresh supply is received, he is to direct that that remaining in the coal-bunkers be, as far as practicable, so stowed as to be used first.

He is, before leaving the port where the vessel was fitted, to cause all the spare gear belonging to the engines and machinery to be taken on board, and he is to land no part of it at any port where he may touch without the written authority of the commanding officer of the station, or of the commander of the squadron to which he belongs.

Whenever he joins his commanding officer after separation, or when he arrives at any port where there is a superior officer in command, he shall report the number of hours the vessel was under steam and under sail, and the circumstances which rendered the use of steam necessary.

When practicable he shall, before going to sea, cause the boilers to be filled with fresh water.

He will direct the engineer to have the flues, chimneys, and boilers cleaned whenever it may be necessary, and when repairs or cleaning are required for the engines and boilers, they are to be made, as far as practicable, by the engineers, firemen, and coal-heavers of the vessel.

He shall take care that the proper lanterns to prevent collisions at sea be kept in good order, and always lighted at night, except when it may be expedient to conceal all lights.

He is to have the force-pumps, hose, and all other means for extinguishing fires, kept constantly in order and ready for immediate use; and he is to require the utmost care to be taken at all times in the storage of stores, the use of lights and fires, and in the adoption of all other precautionary measures to prevent danger from fire.

He shall examine the steam-log daily, and if satisfied of its correctness, sign it every month, or oftener, should the vessel in the mean time arrive at any port.

The commander of the vessel shall transmit to the Department, by the first safe opportunity after the close of the months of March, June, September, and December, a fair copy of the steam log-book for the preceding quarter, and whenever a steamer is placed in ordinary, for the period which has not been previously transmitted.

He will require the engineers to conform to the orders of the officer of the deck for the time being; but they are not, except in cases of necessity, to be ordered to perform other duties than those immediately connected with the preservation, repair, management, or supplying of the engines and their dependencies.

He will cause the engineers, firemen, and coal-heavers to be arranged in watches, and, when on watch, they are to be under the immediate direction of the senior engineer of the watch, and are not to be ordered on other duties than those connected with the engines, boilers, and their dependencies, except in cases of necessity, and then the engineer on duty is to be informed, that he may adopt all necessary precautions.

He will cause the senior engineer to submit for the approval of the executive officer, watch, fire, quarter, and cleaning bills, showing the specific duties of the engineers, firemen, and coal-heavers.

He will require the senior engineer on board to examine daily the engines and their dependencies, and all parts of the vessel which are occupied by them, or by stores for their use, and to report them to the executive officer for inspection; to make immediate report, should any defect or danger be discovered; to give timely notice to the commander of the vessel of the probable wants of his department, and whenever articles are received for it, to carefully examine if they are of proper quality, and report any which, in his opinion, may be objectionable.

He will make such regulations with regard to leave on shore that the ship will never be left without the services of an experienced engineer. He will cause a full engineer watch to be kept constantly whenever the fires are lighted, and take care that one engineer, at least, with a watch of firemen and coal-heavers, are always on hand, even though the ship may be at anchor and the fires hauled. With a reduced complement of engineers this article will be complied with as nearly as may be possible.

Steam may be raised on board vessels of the Navy for the purpose of dispelling damp and unwholesome air or drying the ship, whenever, in the opinion of the commanding officer, it is necessary.

The commanding officer of a vessel having full sail-power will get up steam on his vessel once a month, for the purpose of turning over the engines, and, when practicable, will take an opportunity to do so when going in or out of port.

[GENERAL ORDER.]

NAVY DEPARTMENT,
January 29, 1862.

Whenever any important accident or derangement shall *A survey to be held after accident to machinery.* occur to the machinery of a United States steamer, there shall be held upon it a strict and careful survey by a board composed of one sea officer and at least two engineer officers, which shall report in writing the nature and extent of the accident or derangement, the cause thereof, the probable time of repair, and to whom, if any, blame in connexion therewith is to be attributed. The report is to embrace every detail necessary to a complete understanding of the case. The order of the survey shall accompany the report, which is to be made in duplicate and forwarded to the Department by the first opportunity.

GIDEON WELLES,
Secretary of the Navy.

[Extract from General Order No. 19, dated September 16, 1863.]

Condition o f machinery a test of the engineers' efficiency.

Engineers will hereafter understand that the condition of the machinery under their charge on the arrival of the vessel from a cruise will be considered as a test of their efficiency and fidelity in the discharge of their duties; and that the result of the examination then made will determine whether they have discharged their duties in such a manner as to deserve commendation, or have been so grossly negligent or incompetent as to render their expulsion from the service an act of justice to the public.

GIDEON WELLES.

INSTRUCTIONS TO SUPERINTENDING ENGINEERS.

[CIRCULAR.]

NAVY DEPARTMENT,
January, 1864.

SIR: The great damage which has been sustained by the Navy Department from the poor materials and bad workmanship used by some contractors in the manufacture of its steam machinery, requires that every possible precaution and vigilance on the part of its inspectors should be exercised to prevent their occurrences in the future.

Duties of superintending engineers.

By the specifications you are entitled to demand the best materials that art can furnish, and a degree of workmanship which may be called perfect. It is impossible for the contractor to do more than comply with these specifications; and if, in your opinion, his materials and workmanship admit of improvement, it is your duty to inexorably exact it.

The loss to the Government from badly-built machinery is not to be measured by the money cost thus saved to the contractor. It is immeasurably greater; the giving way of a part in which but a few dollars could be retrenched by the substitution of inferior materials, or the employment of unskillful labor, may involve the loss of the use of a steamer at a time when her services may be worth more than her whole commercial value; in fact, at a time when an event of national importance, not to be measured by money at all, may depend on her efficiency. Your patriotism, as well as your honor, honesty, and professional reputation, is involved in the performance of your duty with inflexible fidelity to the Government, and you are expected to give your whole time and your whole mind to the important work which the Department has committed to your supervision. For any omission or defects arising from neglect of this you wil be considered responsible; and any present made by contractors to any person in the employment of the Department will be viewed by it with strong disapprobation, and the reception of such present will be sufficient cause for removal.

Your attention is particularly called to the following points:

1st. That the boiler plate is of the first quality, highly malleable, ductile and tough, capable of being tightly compressed by the rivets, and of being calked in a durable manner. · It is impossible to make a tight boiler of inferior iron. The rivets should be of the best quality of iron that it is possible to make, and thoroughly worked. The double-riveted seams are to be made true and fair, and calked on both sides. There are but few places where this cannot be done, whereas it is believed there are many cases where it is not done. The rivets are to be staggered, and not placed too far apart. It should be remembered that the principal object of double-riveting in rectangular boilers is tightness, not strength. Neither acids nor "quakers" to be allowed in making the seams.

2nd. The tube plates are to be drilled, not punched, and to the *precise* diameter of the tube, so that the latter fits the hole absolutely tight before being expanded. Immense loss has been inflicted on the Department by some contractors making the tube holes from one thirty-second to two thirty-seconds of an inch too large in order to secure a cheap and easy fit of the tube; and the latter being of too poor material to endure the expansion required to fill a hole so much too large, splits at the ends and leaks ever afterward. This leakage, even at only a few joints, with iron vertical water-tubes, soon destroys all the tubes in the box, the lye formed by the water with the coal-ashes and soot on the lower plate spreading over the entire bottom of the box and rapidly corroding out the lower part of every tube in it. You will be vigilant to see that the diameters of the tube holes are accurate. Nothing is so destructive to a boiler as leaks, and no pains or cost should be spared to prevent them. The socket bolts of the water bottoms should all have heads on the inside, and on the outside large washers and nuts.

3d. As the boilers are intended for carying high steam, and are braced for the same, you will be particular to secure in the crow-feet, half-moons, joints, angle and T iron, pine, &c., and in the riveting by which the braces are attached to the boiler shell, the same strength which the specifications require in the braces. It is obviously useless to make a boiler for high steam and attach its heavy bracing to the shell by a system of riveting with strength inferior to that of the braces.

4th. The quality of the iron for the cylinder and its valve should receive your most anxious scrutiny. It should be of the best scrap, carefully selected, tough, with a fine compact grain, and so hard that the tool can barely work it. The cylinder and its valve must be cast at different times and of different metals. With steam of high pressure and superheated, the greatest care is required in securing the proper quality of metal and workmanship for horizontal cylinders with slide valves. The boring of the cylinder and the facing of the valve and its seat should be perfect.

5th. The main and crank-pin journals must be turned perfectly true from end to end, and highly polished. They must also be mathematically in line and without a flaw.

6th. The brasses for these journals must be of the composition required in the specifications, and you will personally be present and see the metals weighed out in the proper proportions, mixed and poured. They are to be first bored and channeled, and then scraped to their journals. They are to have sufficient end-play to allow for expansions when heated. They are to be closely examined, and, if not of uniform texture, rejected.

7th. You will personally see to the securing of the thrust pillow block, and to the quality and workmanship of its brasses.

8th. You will personally superintend the "lining" of the engine.

9th. You will give particular attention to the tightness of the joints, especially of the vacuum joints, and to the packing of the engine.

10th. The lignum-vitæ in the pump-packings and in the stern-bushings is to be thoroughly soaked before being bored to the required diameter.

It is to be distinctly understood by you that there are to be no variations from the requirements of the contracts, nor any additions thereto unless authorized by the proper Bureau, with a copy of which you must be furnished by the general superintendent.

I am, very respectfully, your obedient servant,

GIDEON WELLES,
Secretary of the Navy.

RANK.

AN ACT to establish and equalize the grades of line officers of the United States Navy.

*　　　*　　　*　　　*　　　*　　　*

Relative rank between officers of the Army and Navy.

SEC. 13. *And be it further enacted,* That the relative rank between officers of the Navy and the Army shall be as follows, lineal rank only to be considered:

Rear-admirals with major generals.
Commodores with brigadier generals.
Captains with colonels.
Commanders with lieutenant colonels.
Lieutenant commanders with majors.
Lieutenants with captains.
Masters with first lieutenants.
Ensigns with second lieutenants.

*　　　*　　　*　　　*　　　*　　　*

Approved July 16, 1862. (Vol. 12, p. 583.)

AN ACT making appropriations for the naval service for the year ending June thirty, eighteen hundred and seventy-two, and for other purposes.

*　　　　*　　　　*　　　　*　　　　*　　　　*

SEC. 7. That the officers of the Engineer Corps on the active list of the Navy shall be as follows:

Ten chief engineers, who shall have the relative rank of captain;

Fifteen chief engineers, who shall have the relative rank of commander; and

Forty-five chief engineers, who shall have the relative rank of lieutenant commander or lieutenant;

And each and all of the above-named officers of the Engineer Corps shall have the pay of chief engineers of the Navy, as now provided.

One hundred first assistant engineers, who shall have the relative rank of lieutenant or master; and

One hundred second assistant engineers, who shall have the relative rank of master or ensign; and the said assistant engineers shall have the pay of first and second assistant engineers of the Navy, respectively, as now provided.

*　　　　*　　　　*　　　　*　　　　*　　　　*

SEC. 8. That no person under nineteen or over twenty-six years of age shall be appointed a second assistant engineer in the Navy; nor shall any person be appointed or promoted in the engineer corps until after he has been found qualified by a board of competent engineer and medical officers designated by the Secretary of the Navy, and has complied with existing regulations.

*　　　　*　　　　*　　　　*　　　　*　　　　*

SEC. 10. That the foregoing grades, hereby established for the staff corps of the Navy, shall be filled by appointment from the highest numbers in each corps, according to seniority, and that new commissions shall be issued to the officers so appointed, in which commissions the titles and grades herein established shall be inserted; and no existing commission shall be vacated in the said several staff corps except by the issue of new commissions, required by the provisions of this act, and no officer shall be reduced in rank or lose seniority in his own corps by any change which may be required under the provisions of this act; and the officers of the staff corps of the Navy shall take precedence in their several corps, and in their several grades, and with officers of the line with whom they hold relative rank, according to length of service in the Navy: *Provided*, That, in estimating the length of service for this purpose, the several officers of the staff corps shall, respectively, take precedence in their several grades, and with those officers of the line of the Navy with whom they hold relative rank who have been in the naval service six years longer than such officers of said staff corps have been in said service: *And provided further*, That, in estimating such length of service, officers who have been advanced or lost numbers on the Navy Register shall be considered as having gained or lost length of service accordingly.

*　　　　*　　　　*　　　　*　　　　*　　　　*

Rank of Chief of Bureau.

SEC. 12. That the chief of the Bureau * * * of Steam Engineering shall have the relative rank of commodore while holding said position, (or if heretofore or hereafter retired therefrom by reason of age or length of service.)* * *
Approved March 3, 1871.

PRECEDENCE.

AN ACT making appropriations for the naval service for the year ending June thirty, eighteen hundred and seventy-two, and for other purposes.

Precedence according to rank.

SEC. 12. * * * * That commanding officers of vessels of war and of naval stations shall take precedence over all officers placed under their command, and the Secretary of the Navy may, in his discretion, detail a line officer to act as the aid or executive of the commanding officer of a vessel of war, or naval station, which officer shall, when not impracticable, be next in rank to said commanding officer, and who, as such aid or executive, shall, while executing the orders of the commanding officer, on board such vessel, or at such station, take precedence over all officers attached to such vessel or station; and all orders of such aid or executive shall be regarded as proceeding from the commanding officer; and such aid or executive shall have no independent authority in consequence of such detail; and staff officers, senior to the officer so detailed, shall have the right to communicate directly with the commanding officer, and in processions on shore, on courts-martial, summary courts, courts of inquiry, boards of survey, and all other boards, line and staff officers shall take precedence according to rank.

SEC. 13. That all acts and parts of acts inconsistent with this act are hereby repealed.

Approved March 3, 1871.

PROMOTION, &c.

AN ACT to amend an act entitled "An act to establish and equalize the grade of line officers of the United States Navy," approved July sixteen, eighteen hundred and sixty-two.

Officers below grade of commodore not to be promoted until mental, moral, and professional fitness is established, &c.

Be it enacted by the Senate and House of Representatives of the United States of America in Congress assembled, That no line officer of the Navy upon the active list, below the grade of commodore, nor any other naval officer, shall be promoted to a higher grade until his mental, moral, and professional fitness to perform all his duties at sea shall be established to the satisfaction of a board of examining officers to be appointed by the President of the United States. And such board shall have power to take testimony, the witnesses when present to be sworn by the president of the board, and to examine all matter on the files and records of the Department in relation to any officer whose case shall be considered by them.

SEC. 2. *And be it further enacted*, That such examining board shall consist of not less than three officers, senior in rank to the officer to be examined. *Examining board—of whom composed.*

SEC. 3. *And be it further enacted*, That any officer to be acted upon by said board shall have the right to be present, if he desires it; and his statement of his case, on oath, and the testimony of witnesses, and his examination shall be recorded. *Rights of the officer to be acted upon.*

*　　*　　*　　*　　*　　*

SEC. 4. *And be it further enacted*, That no officer in the naval service shall be promoted to a higher grade therein, upon the active list, until he has been examined by a board of naval surgeons, and pronounced physically qualified to perform all his duties at sea. And all officers whose cases shall have been acted upon by the aforesaid boards, and who shall not have been recommended for promotion by both of them, shall be placed upon the retired list. *Promotion to higher grade—examination required.* *Officers not recommended, to be retired.*

*　　*　　*　　*　　*　　*

Approved April 21, 1864.   (Vol. 13, p. 53.)

AN ACT to provide for an advance of rank to officers of the Navy and Marine Corps for distinguished merit.

Be it enacted by the Senate and House of Representatives of the United States of America in Congress assembled, That any officer of the Navy or Marine Corps, by and with the advice and consent of the Senate, may be advanced not exceeding thirty numbers in rank, for having exhibited eminent and conspicuous conduct in battle, or extraordinary heroism. *Advancement of officers of Navy and of Marine Corps for conspicuous conduct in battle.*

SEC. 2. *And be it further enacted*, That any officer of the Navy or Marine Corps, either of volunteers or otherwise, who shall be nominated to a higher grade by the provisions of the first section of this act, or of that of section nine of an act entitled "An act to establish and equalize the grades of line officers of the United States Navy," approved July sixteenth, eighteen hundred and sixty-two, shall be promoted, notwithstanding the number of said grade may be full, but no further promotions shall take place in that grade, except for like cause, until the number is reduced to that provided by law. *Promotion of officers of Navy and Marine Corps nominated to a higher grade.* *Restriction.*

*　　*　　*　　*　　*

Approved January 24, 1865.   (Vol. 13, p. 424.)

[Extract from an act to prevent officers of the Navy from being deprived of their regular promotion on account of wounds received in battle, and for other purposes.]

Be it enacted by the Senate and House of Representatives of the United States of America in Congress assembled, That the provision of section four of the act to amend an act entitled "An act to establish and equalize the grade of line officers *Officers not to be deprived of promotion on account of wounds received in battle.*

of the United States Navy," approved July sixteen, eighteen hundred and sixty-two, requiring that no officer in the naval service shall be promoted to a higher grade upon the active list until he has been examined by a board of naval surgeons and pronounced physically qualified to perform all his duties at sea, shall not be construed to apply to, and exclude from the promotion to which he would otherwise be regularly entitled, any officer in whose case such medical board shall report that his physical disqualification was occasioned by wounds received in the line of his duty, and that such wounds do not incapacitate him for other duties in the grade to which he shall be promoted.

* * * * * *

Approved July 28, 1866.

For the promotion of officers on the retired and reserved lists, see "Retired Officers," p. 58.

QUARTERS.

Rooms on starboard side of ward-room for line officers, on port side for staff officers. The state-rooms on the starboard side of the ward-room are to be occupied by the line officers, and those on the port side by the staff officers of the ward-room mess. * *

Forward room on port side for engineer in charge. On the port side, the forward state-room of all connected with the ward-room is to be occupied by the senior engineer on board in charge of the engines. * * * *

GIDEON WELLES,
Secretary of the Navy.

NAVY DEPARTMENT, *March* 13, 1868.

[CIRCULAR.]

NAVY DEPARTMENT,
October 3, 1871.

The following modifications of, and additions to, previous regulations and circulars are hereby ordered:

OCCUPATION OF ROOMS.

In 1st and 2d class vessels rooms in the ward-room will be occupied as follows:

Starboard side.

Forward room . . . . Executive officer.
Next aft . . . . Navigation and ordnance officer.
All rooms abaft these by . . . . Line officers according to rank.

Port side.

Forward room . . . . Chief engineer.
Next aft . . . . Paymaster.
Next aft . . . . Surgeon.
Next aft . . . . Senior marine offier.
Next aft . . . . Chaplain.
Next aft . . . . Secretary.
All rooms abaft these by . . . . Staff officers according to rank.

UNIFORM.

Masters will wear the epaulets, cocked hat, and shoulder-straps prescribed for officers of that grade in the Uniform Regulations of December 1, 1866.

The uniform to be worn by a secretary to a commander-in-chief of a fleet or commander of a squadron will be as prescribed in the Regulations of December 1, 1866.

GEO. M. ROBESON,
Secretary of the Navy.

EXTRACTS FROM REGULATIONS PRESCRIBING THE UNIFORM FOR THE UNITED STATES NAVY.

GENERAL REGULATIONS.

Full-dress uniform for occasions of special ceremony.—Body-coat as prescribed, epaulets, cocked hat, sword with sword-knot, and blue-cloth or white-drilling pantaloons, to suit the season of the year, weather, or climate, as may be directed by the senior officer present.

Full-dress uniform for general duty and official visits on shore.—Frock-coat as prescribed, epaulets, cocked hat or cap, sword with sword-knot, and blue-cloth or white-drilling pantaloons, to suit the season of the year, weather, or climate, as may be directed by the senior officer present.

Service dress and undress uniform.—Frock-coat as prescribed, with shoulder-straps, cap, and with or without sword and sword-knot; pantaloons, blue or white, to suit the season of the year, weather, or climate, as may be directed by the senior officer present.

Officers will wear the prescribed full-dress uniform for " occasions of special ceremony," whenever they make special official visits of ceremony to the President, or Secretary of the Navy, or to foreign authorities and vessels of war.

Officers will wear either the prescribed full-dress uniform for "general duty" or the " undress uniform" whenever they make official visits to the President, Secretary of the Navy, heads of other Departments, or to foreign authorities and vessels of war.

Officers serving on courts-martial, courts of inquiry, boards of examination, or special boards, or when attending as witnesses before courts-martial or courts of inquiry, or in any other capacity, will wear the undress uniform, without swords, unless otherwise specially directed by competent authority.

Officers in their social intercourse within the United States (upon occasions requiring them to appear in evening dress) may wear a body-coat made according to the prevailing fashion, of Navy-blue cloth, with five Navy buttons on each breast, and with the devices of rank and grade on the ends of the collar, as authorized for sack and overcoats, but without shoulder-straps, epaulets, cocked hat, or sleeve ornaments.

It is optional with officers to wear their uniform while on duty in the Navy Department, at the Observatory, Hydrographic Office, or on Light-house duty ashore.

Undress uniform is to be worn by all officers when attached to any vessel of the Navy or Coast Survey, to any navy-yard or station, or to any hospital or other naval establishment, for duty, unless when absent on leave.

Swords are always to be worn at quarters, and on leaving a vessel, navy-yard, or station, on military duty.

Officers on furlough will not wear their uniform, and officers are strictly prohibited from wearing any part of it while suspended from duty by sentence of a court-martial.

Chaplains, when performing divine service, may wear either the vestments of the church to which they belong or the uniform prescribed in the regulations.

On all occasions of ceremony or duty, abroad or in the United States, when a commanding officer may deem it necessary to order the attendance of the officers under his command, he shall be careful in such order to prescribe the particular dress to be worn.

Officers attached to vessels in foreign ports will not visit the shore without being in uniform, except by permission of commanding officer.

Officers are forbidden to wear any part of their uniform with citizens' dress. They must wear the whole of their uniform or none.

Before a vessel proceeds to sea there will be a general muster for the purpose of ascertaining whether the officers and crew are provided with the uniform, full and undress, as prescribed by the regulations, and the commanding officer of the vessel will see that all deficiencies are supplied.

DRESS.

Full-dress body-coat.

The full-dress body-coat for the admiral, vice-admiral, rear-admirals, commodores, captains, commanders, lieutenant commanders, lieutenants, masters, ensigns, and all staff officers of relative rank, respectively, shall be of Navy-blue cloth, double-breasted, lined with white silk serge; the waist of the coat to descend to the top of the hip-bone; the skirts to begin about one-fifth of the circumference from the front edge and descend four-fifths from the hip-bone toward the knee, with one button behind on each hip, and one near the bottom of the pocket in each fold; two rows of large Navy buttons on the breast, nine in each row, placed four inches and a half apart from eye to eye at top, and two inches and a half at bottom; the cuffs of the coat to be closed, without buttons, and to be from two and a half to three inches deep; standing collar to hook in front at bottom, and to slope thence upward and backward at an angle of twenty-five degrees on each side, and to rise no higher than will permit a free movement of the chin over it; to have one strip of gold-embroidered white-oak leaves (as per pattern) for the admiral, vice-admiral, and rear-admirals; to have a strip of Navy gold lace one inch wide around the top and down the front for commodores, captains, and commanders, and one-half inch wide for lieutenant commanders, lieutenants, masters, and ensigns.

All staff officers will wear the same widths of gold lace around the top and down the front of the collars of their full-dress body-coats as prescribed for line officers, with whom they have relative rank, respectively.

*   *   *   *   *   *   *

The full-dress body-coat is to be worn only with epaulets, cocked hat, sword, and sword-knot.

*   *   *   *   *   *   *

Full-dress duty, undress, and service frock-coat.

The full-dress duty, undress, and service frock-coat for all commissioned officers will be of Navy-blue cloth, faced with the same, and lined with black silk serge; double-breasted, with two rows of large Navy buttons on the breast, nine in each row, placed four inches and a half apart from eye to eye at top, and two inches and a half at bottom; rolling collar; skirts to be full, commencing at the hip-bone and descending four-fifths thence toward the knee, with one button behind on each hip and one near the bottom of the pocket in each fold; cuffs to be closed, without buttons, and from two and a half to three inches deep.

*　　*　　*　　*　　*　　*　　*

Sack-coats.

Sack-coats of Navy-blue flannel or blue cloth may be worn off duty by all officers on board ship and in the United States; but never on shore, nor on board ship on duty in a foreign port. Sack-coats shall be single-breasted, with a row of five medium-size buttons on the right breast. Shoulder-straps and lace on the sleeves will be dispensed with on sack-coats—retaining the star for line officers—in which case the designations of rank and corps will be worn on the ends of the collar, as follows:

*　　*　　*　　*　　*　　*　　*

Commodores.—One silver star, with a silver anchor back of it.
Captains.—A silver spread-eagle, with a silver anchor back of it.
Commanders.—A silver leaf, with a silver anchor back of it.
Lieutenant Commanders.—A gold leaf, with a silver anchor back of it.
Lieutenants.—Two gold bars, with a silver anchor back of them.
Masters.—One gold bar, with a silver anchor back of it.
Ensigns.—A silver anchor placed horizontally stock up.
Midshipmen.—A gold cord, one-eighth of an inch in diameter and one and one-quarter of an inch long, across the end of the collar.

Staff officers will wear on the ends of the collars of their sack-coats their respective shoulder-strap devices in the same way as the line officers with whom they have relative rank, omitting the duplicate end device.

*　　*　　*　　*　　*　　*

Pantaloons.

For all officers, are to be of Navy-blue cloth or white duck or drilling, (or for " service dress," of navy-blue flannel.)

Within the tropics white pantaloons are to be worn at all seasons of the year, unless otherwise ordered by the officer in command.

North of the tropics blue pantaloons are to be worn from the 1st of October to the 15th of May, and white ones from the 15th of May to the 1st of October, when the weather is suitable; and south of the tropics *vice versa,* subject, however, to such exceptions as may be directed or authorized by the senior officer present in command.

Vests.

For all officers, will be single-breasted, standing collar, with nine small Navy buttons in front, and made of Navy-blue cloth, fine blue flannel, or of suitable white material.

Jackets and flannel coats.

Jackets may be worn as "service dress" by all officers, except at general muster, or upon special occasions of ceremony, when a different dress is prescribed by the commanding officer; to be of Navy-blue cloth, faced with the same, and lined with black silk serge; double or single breasted, as in the coat; rolling collar, with the same number of small-sized buttons on the breast as for the coat, and with the same arrangement of lace on the cuffs, and the same shoulder-straps.

In mild climates or seasons, officers in "service dress" may wear the uniform made of Navy-blue fine flannel. Coats to be lined with black silk serge, and furnished with Navy buttons of medium size. The same may be worn on shipboard at sea, except at general muster; also on board ship in port, except at general muster, when on watch with the colors hoisted, or on occasions of ceremony, when a different dress is prescribed by the commanding officer.

White linen or grass jackets, to be made like the cloth ones, but without straps or sleeve ornaments, may be worn within the tropics, at sea and in port, with white straw hats, when the weather, in the opinion of the commanding officer, is such as to require it. They must not, however, be worn ashore in foreign ports, nor by the officer of the deck, for the time being, in ports where the vessel may be visited by strangers.

Overcoats.

Overcoats shall be a caban overcoat and cape, of dark-blue beaver or pilot cloth, skirt to extend below the knee; cape to be ten inches shorter; double-breasted, with pockets in side seam, and five Navy buttons on each breast. The cape to be made so that it can be removed at pleasure, so as to form a separate garment. On each end of the collar of the overcoat the same devices of rank and corps shall be worn, respectively, as authorized for sack-coats.

*　　　*　　　*　　　*　　　*　　　*　　　*

Cravat.

Cravat for all officers, to be of black silk or satin, with a white shirt-collar showing above it.

SLEEVE ORNAMENTS.

*　　　*　　　*　　　*　　　*　　　*　　　*

Full-dress body and frock-coats.

For commodores, one strip of gold lace, two inches wide, one inch and a half from the edge of the sleeve.

For captains, four strips of Navy gold lace one-half inch wide, one-quarter of an inch apart; the lower strip one inch and a half from the lower edge of the sleeve.

For commanders, the same, except that there shall be but three strips of gold lace.

For lieutenant commanders, the same, except that there shall be but two strips of gold lace.

For lieutenants, the same, except that there shall be but one strip of half-inch gold lace, and one strip of one-quarter-inch gold lace, one-quarter of an inch above it.

For a master, the same, except that there shall be but one strip of half-inch gold lace.

For an ensign, the same, except that there will be but one strip of one quarter-inch gold lace.

Staff officers of assimilated rank will conform to the above.

*   *   *   *   *   *   *

Engineers will wear around the sleeve red cloth, between the strips of gold lace.

Staff officers entitled to but one strip of lace on the sleeve will wear the colored cloth so as to show one-fourth of an inch above and below the strip.

No other officers are entitled to wear the above-described ornaments.

EPAULETS, SHOULDER-STRAPS, ETC.

Epaulets.

All commissioned officers, including and above the rank of lieutenant, will wear two gold-bullion epaulets with their respective strap ornaments on the frogs, to be of the following dimensions:

For the admiral, vice-admiral, rear-admirals, and commodores, the strap to be two and three-quarters of an inch wide and six inches long; frog four and three-eighths of an inch wide; crescent eleven-sixteenths of an inch in the broadest part; bullion three and one-half inches long and five-eighths of an inch in diameter. Staff officers of relative rank to wear the same.

For captains, commanders, lieutenant commanders, and staff officers of relative rank, the strap to be two and three-quarters of an inch wide and six inches long; frog four and three-eighths of an inch wide; crescent eleven-sixteenths of an inch in the broadest part; bullion three inches long and half an inch in diameter.

For lieutenants and staff officers of relative rank, the strap to be two and one-half inches wide and six inches long; frog four and three-eighths of an inch wide; crescent nine-sixteenths of an inch in the broadest part; bullion three inches long and three-eighths of an inch in diameter.

Shoulder-straps.

No officer in the Navy below the assimilated rank of lieutenant will wear shoulder-straps, cocked hat, or epaulets.

Masters, ensigns, and midshipmen, after graduation, and staff officers of assimilated rank, will wear, in lieu of shoulder-straps or epaulets, gold-embroidered shoulder-loops as per patterns; staff officers omitting the anchor.

These can also be worn on the undress frock-coat, either on duty or on other occasions.

All shoulder-straps are to be of Navy-blue cloth, four inches and a quarter long, and one inch and a half wide, including the border, which is to be a quarter of an inch wide and embroidered in gold, except for the admiral, which will be four and seven-eighths inches long and one and five-eighths of an inch wide, including the border, which is to be one-quarter of an inch wide.

The center and end ornaments, or distinctions of the line and staff, and indications of rank, are to be embroidered in gold or in silver, as hereinafter designated, and are to be as follows:

3 E C

Devices for shoulder-straps and frogs of epaulets.

* * * * * * *

For commodores, a silver star of five rays, placed in the center, with a silver foul anchor at each end of the strap, or frog of the epaulet.

For captains, a silver spread-eagle in the center, with a silver foul anchor at each end of the strap, or frog of the epaulet.

For commanders, a silver oak-leaf at each end, with a silver foul anchor in the center of the strap, or frog of the epaulet.

For lieutenant commanders, a gold oak-leaf at each end, with a silver foul anchor in the center of the strap, or frog of the epaulet.

For lieutenants, two gold bars at each end, with a silver foul anchor in the center of the strap, or frog of the epaulet.

Staff officers will wear shoulder-straps of the same description as prescribed for line officers with whom they have relative rank, respectively, with the following exceptions, viz:

* * * * * * *

In the Engineers' Corps a device of four oak-leaves in the form of a cross is substituted.

* * * * * * *

COCKED HAT, CAP, ETC.

Cocked hat.

All commissioned officers, including and above the rank of lieutenant, will wear a black cocked hat of the following dimensions:

To be not more than six nor less than five and a half inches on the back fan; and not more than five and a half nor less than five inches on the front fan; and not more than eighteen nor less than sixteen inches long from peak to peak. The hat to be bound with black-silk lace, to show one inch and a quarter on each side. In the fold, at each end of the hat, a tassel will be worn, formed of five gold and five blue bullions; and on the front or right fan, a black-silk cockade four and a half inches in diameter.

The admiral, vice-admiral, rear-admirals, commodores, and staff officers of relative rank, will wear over the cockade a loop of six gold bullions, half an inch in diameter, the two inner bullions to be twisted together, with a small Navy button in the lower end of the loop.

All other officers entitled to wear cocked hats will wear over the cockade a loop formed of four gold bullions, three-eighths of an inch in diameter, not twisted, with a small Navy button in the lower end of the loop.

Cap.

The cap to be of dark blue cloth; diameter of the top to be the same as the base; quarters not less than one and a quarter nor more than one-inch and a half wide in front, sloping gradually; and to be not less than one-half nor more than three-quarters of an inch wide at the back of the cap. The seam around the tip to be without a welt, and neatly stitched on each side. Band to be one inch and a half wide, with a welt one-eighth of an inch in diameter at the top, and a welt one-eighth of an inch in diameter one-quarter of an inch from the base of the cap. A plain black-ribbed silk band will be worn between the upper and lower welts. Visor to be of black patent leather, bound green underneath, and not less than one and a half nor more than one and three-quarters of an inch wide in front, and rounded, as per pattern. The inside band to be of stout pasteboard, and to extend from the base of the cap to within one-quarter of an inch of the tip. The sweat and inside linings to be of uncolored morocco. The cap in front is to be not less than two and a half nor more than three inches in height, according to size, with four black metal eyelets inserted in the top for ventilation.

During rainy weather only a black glazed silk cover may be worn over the cap.

Cap ornaments.

The cap ornament for all commissioned officers in the Navy and midshipmen after graduation will be a silver shield with two crossed anchors in gold, arranged as per pattern. A gold cord of the same pattern as the one now worn by the midshipmen at the Naval Academy will be worn on the front of the cap by all officers.

Straw hats.

In tropical climates, or during warm seasons, officers may wear white straw hats under the same restrictions as in the case of jackets; the body of the hat to be not more than three and a half nor less than two and a half inches in height, and the brim, without lining, not more than three and a half nor less than two inches in width, with a plain band of black ribbon.

SWORDS, ETC.

Sword and scabbard.

For all officers, shall be a cut-and-thrust blade, not less than twenty-six nor more than twenty-nine inches long; half-basket hilt; grip, white; scabbards of black leather; mountings of yellow gilt; and all as per pattern.

The full-dress sword-belt of the admiral, vice-admiral, rear-admirals, and commodores will be of blue cloth, with a small gold cord around the edge, and one strip of gold-embroidered white-oak leaves, one-half inch wide, running through the center, as per pattern.

The sling-straps to be of blue cloth, with a small gold thread around the edge, as per pattern.

The full-dress sword-belts of the different grades below the rank of commodore will be of blue webbing, with gold cord woven in, as per patterns.

*   *   *   *   *   *

Undress sword-belt.

For all officers, shall be of plain black glazed leather, not less than one inch and a half nor more than two inches wide, with slings of the same not less than one-half nor more than three-quarters of an inch wide, and a hook in the forward ring to suspend the sword. Belt-plate of yellow gilt in front, two inches in diameter; the belt to be worn over the coat.

Sword-knot.

For all officers, except mates, clerks, boatswains, gunners, carpenters, and sail-makers, shall be a strap of gold lace twenty-four inches long, including the tassel, gold slide, tassel of twelve gold bullions, one inch and three-quarters long, inclosing five blue bullions, with basket-worked head.

Buttons.

Shall be gilt, convex, and of three sizes in exterior diameter; large, seven-eighths of an inch; medium, seven-tenths of an inch; and small, nine-sixteenths of an inch. Each size is to have the same device.

PETTY OFFICERS, SEAMEN, ETC.

Uniform dress for petty officers, seamen, firemen, coal-heavers, ordinary seamen, landsmen, and boys.

Seamen, gunners, machinists, masters-at-arms, yeomen, apothecaries, and paymasters' writers will wear blue jackets, with rolling collars, double-breasted; two rows of medium-size Navy buttons on the breast, six in each row; slashed sleeves or cuffs, with three small-size Navy buttons; plain blue caps, with visor. They will be allowed to wear white cotton or linen shirts (in place of duck frocks, with turn-over collars) and uniform vests, with six small-size Navy buttons.

*　　　*　　　*　　　*　　　*　　　*

Machinists will (in addition to the petty officers' device on the sleeve above the elbow) wear on both sleeves, in front, half-way between the edge of the sleeve and the elbow, a badge representing a paddle-wheel, with a five-pointed star above; to be worked in, or made of white or blue sewing materials, according to the color of the garment—the white upon blue garments, and *vice versa*.

*　　　*　　　*　　　*　　　*　　　*

All line petty officers will wear on their right sleeve above the elbow, in front, an eagle and anchor, of not more than two inches in length, with a star of one inch in diameter one inch above it, the whole to be placed vertically, and made of or worked in white or blue sewing materials, according to the color of the garment—the white upon blue garments, and *vice versa*.

All other petty officers, and first-class firemen, except officers' stewards, will wear the same device on the left sleeve, but without the star.

The outside clothing for petty officers not previously specified, seamen, firemen, and coal-heavers, ordinary seamen, landsmen, and boys, for muster, shall consist of blue-cloth jackets and trowsers, or blue-woolen frocks; blue-cloth caps, without visors; cap-bands to be of black ribbon, one and one-quarter of an inch wide, with the name of the vessel to which they are attached painted on them in yellow or gilt letters.

In warm weather, or within the tropics, it shall consist of white linen or duck frocks, and blue or white trowsers; blue-cloth caps, without visors, or white sennit hats, as the commanding officer may direct; hat or cap bands to be of black ribbon, with the name of the vessel to which they are attached painted on them, as prescribed above; black silk neckerchiefs, and shoes or boots, properly cleaned.

The outside of the collars of all frocks for petty officers, and other enlisted men, will be made of or covered with blue dungaree, or blue nankin; the collars of all frocks to be uniform in size—to be six and one-half inches deep, and with square corners, with a white-embroidered five-pointed star, three-quarters of an inch in diameter, in each corner. No tape on the collars.

The collars to be neatly stitched with white thread—two rows, one-eighth of an inch apart, the first row close to the edge.

The shoulder-pieces of shirts to be doubled; the seams to be over-lapped and double-stitched: the rows of the stitching to be one-half inch apart. The breasts of the shirt to be of double thickness, four inches wide on each side; to be neatly stitched with white thread—two rows of stitching one-half inch apart. The opening in front of the shirt shall extend downward from the collar ten inches, neatly stitched and strengthened at the point where the opening ends. Three tape ties on each side, at equal distances apart; ties to be twelve inches long.

Trowsers are to be made with broad flaps, to button one and three-quarters of an inch from the top.

The cuffs of all frocks to be uniform in length; there will be no dungaree cuffs. The cuffs are to be of the same material as the frocks; to be neatly stitched all around, with two buttons on the sleeve.

Those for landsmen, coal-heavers, and boys shall have one strip of blue dungaree or blue tape around the cuff, one-half inch wide, one inch and one-half from the lower edge.

For ordinary seamen and second-class firemen, two strips, one-quarter of an inch apart; for seamen, three strips; and for petty officers, four strips. On the blue frocks there shall be strips of white tape, one-half inch wide, sewed on in the same manner.

*　　　*　　　*　　　*　　　*　　　*

Caps for all petty officers not otherwise specified, and for enlisted men, will be uniform, both in shape and color, and in the length of bow to the draw-ribbon. White linen cap-covers may be worn within the tropics and elsewhere in very hot weather; the cap-covers to be made a plain circle, a little larger than the circumference of the cap, with a neat white cord, or narrow tape draw-string; and, when tied on the cap, to be not more than half an inch below the rounded part of the top of the cap. The draw-string is to be fastened behind in a small neat knot.

All sennit hats are to be uniform in shape; the height of the crown to be two and one-half inches; the brim to be three inches in width, and without lining.

Hat-ribbons are to be one inch and a quarter wide, and must be uniform, both in width and in length of tie-bow. The lettering is to be of gilt or yellow color, and must be the same in character and size for the whole ship's company.

Petty officers and others who have received "medals of honor" from the Secretary of the Navy will be encouraged to wear them at general muster, and on all other suitable occasions. They will also be allowed to wear a star, from three-quarters to seven-eighths of an inch in diameter, on the left breast of their frocks and jackets, as a distinction.

All enlisted men to wear, on proper occasions, a working-suit, to consist of a jumper and pair of overalls, made of canvas-duck.

The frocks (blue and white) are to be furnished by the paymasters, so as to conform in design with the foregoing uniform, with the exception of the sleeve and cuff marks.

Watch-marks.

The first part of the watch will wear one bar made of white tape or blue material, according to the color of the frock, one-half of an inch wide and one inch and a quarter long, to be placed horizontally on the front part of the sleeve, one inch below the shoulder-seam.

The second part of the watch will wear two bars, one-half an inch apart, parallel to each other and placed horizontally, the upper bar to be one inch below the shoulder-seam.

The starboard watch will wear the watch-marks on the right arm, and the port watch will wear them on the left arm.

Petty officers, with special arm devices indicating starboard and port watches, will not be required to wear other watch-marks.

It is strictly enjoined upon commandants of stations, and commanding officers of the Navy, to see that the foregoing regulations are complied with in every respect, and to require all deviations from them to be corrected.

GEORGE M. ROBESON,
Secretary of the Navy.

NAVY DEPARTMENT, *July* 14, 1869.

That officers on the retired and reserved lists may wear the uniform of their respective grades, see p. 58.

PAY AND EMOLUMENTS.

AN ACT making appropriations for the naval service for the year ending June thirtieth, eighteen hundred and seventy-one, and for other purposes.

* * * * * *

Pay, when to commence. SEC. 7. *And be it further enacted,* That the pay of an officer of the Navy, upon his original entry into the service, except where he is required to give an official bond, shall commence upon the date of his acceptance of his appointment; * * * Increased pay, when to commence. that hereafter the increased pay of a promoted officer shall commence from the date he is to take rank as stated in his commission. * * * * *

Approved July 15, 1870.

AN ACT making appropriations for the naval service for the year ending June thirty, eighteen hundred and seventy-two, and for other purposes.

Pay of Chief of Bureau. SEC. 12. * * * That the pay of Chiefs of Bureau in the Navy Department shall be the highest pay of the grade to which they belong, but not below that of commodore. * * * * *

Approved March 3, 1871.

AN ACT making appropriations for the naval service for the year ending June thirtieth, eighteen hundred and seventy-one, and for other purposes.

*　　　*　　　*　　　*　　　*　　　*

SEC. 3. *And be it further enacted*, That from and after the thirtieth day of June, eighteen hundred and seventy, the annual pay of the officers of the Navy on the active list shall be as follows: Annual pay of engineers on the active list.

*　　　*　　　*　　　*　　　*　　　*

Fleet surgeons, fleet paymasters, and fleet engineers, four thousand four hundred dollars. Of fleet engineers.

Surgeons, paymasters, and chief engineers during the first five years after date of commission, when at sea, two thousand eight hundred dollars; on shore duty, two thousand four hundred dollars; on leave or waiting orders, two thousand dollars; during the second five years after such date, when at sea, three thousand two hundred dollars; on shore duty, two thousand eight hundred dollars; on leave or waiting orders, two thousand four hundred dollars; during the third five years after such date, when at sea, three thousand five hundred dollars; on shore duty, three thousand two hundred dollars; on leave or waiting orders, two thousand six hundred dollars; during the fourth five years after such date, when at sea, three thousand seven hundred dollars; on shore duty, three thousand six hundred dollars; on leave or waiting orders, two thousand eight hundred dollars; after twenty years from such date, when at sea, four thousand two hundred dollars; on shore duty, four thousand dollars; on leave or waiting orders, three thousand dollars. Of chief engineers during the first five years. During the second five years. During the third five years. During the fourth five years. After twenty years.

Passed assistant surgeons, passed assistant paymasters, and first assistant engineers, during the first five years after date of appointment, when at sea, two thousand dollars; on shore duty, one thousand eight hundred dollars; on leave or waiting orders, one thousand five hundred dollars; after five years from such date, when at sea, two thousand two hundred dollars; on shore duty, two thousand dollars; on leave or waiting orders, one thousand seven hundred dollars. Of first assistant engineers during the first five years. After five years.

Assistant surgeons, assistant paymasters, and second assistant engineers, during the first five years after date of appointment, when at sea, one thousand seven hundred dollars; *one* [on] shore duty, one thousand four hundred dollars; on leave or waiting orders, one thousand dollars; after five years from such date, when at sea, one thousand nine hundred dollars; on shore duty, one thousand six hundred dollars; on leave or waiting orders, one thousand two hundred dollars. Of second assistant engineers during the first five years. After five years.

SEC. 4. *And be it further enacted*, That the pay prescribed in the next preceding section shall be the full and entire compensation of the several officers therein named, and no additional allowance shall be made in favor of any of said officers on any account whatever, and all laws or parts of laws authorizing any such allowance shall, on the first day of July, eighteen hundred and seventy, be repealed; but this shall not be construed as repealing existing laws allowing rations and traveling expenses to officers; and their No allowance in addition to pay. Except traveling expenses and rations.

traveling expenses in foreign countries shall be considered to include such expenses of transportation of baggage as were necessarily incurred; but no charge for transportation of baggage in connection with travel in the United States shall be allowed.

Approved July 15, 1870.

AN ACT making appropriations for the naval service for the year ending the thirtieth June, one thousand eight hundred and forty-eight.

* * * * * *

President to fix pay of firemen and coal-heavers.

SEC. 4. *And be it further enacted,* That the pay of firemen and coal-heavers employed in the naval service shall hereafter be fixed by the President of the United States, in the same manner as is now provided by law for the pay of other petty officers, and of seamen, ordinary seamen, and marines.

* * * * * *

Approved March 3, 1847.

Back pay.

That officers may receive back pay when dated back after a delayed examination, see p. 13.

FURLOUGH PAY.

AN ACT to regulate the pay of the Navy of the United States.

* * * * * *

Officers on furlough.

And all officers so furloughed shall receive one-half only of the pay to which they would have been entitled if on leave of absence.

* * * * * *

Approved March 3, 1835.

RETIRED PAY.

AN ACT to amend certain acts in relation to the Navy.

* * * * * *

Retired and reserved officers entitled to promotion.

SEC. 9. *And be it further enacted,* That officers on the retired and reserved lists of the Navy shall be entitled to promotion as their several dates upon the active list are promoted; but such promotion shall not entitle them to any pay beyond that to which they were entitled when retired, unless upon active duty, when they shall receive the full pay of their respective grades.

Retired officers on active duty to receive full pay.

* * * * * *

Approved March 2, 1867.

AN ACT making appropriations for the naval service for the year ending June thirtieth, eighteen hundred and seventy-one, and for other purposes.

* * * * * *

Retired officers not on active duty to receive one-half pay.

SEC. 5. *And be it further enacted,* That from and after the thirtieth day of June, eighteen hundred and seventy, the pay of all officers of the Navy now on or hereafter placed on the retired list shall, when not on active duty, be equal to one-half of the highest pay prescribed by this act for officers on the active list whose grade corresponds to the grade held by such retired officers respectively at the time of such retirement, and no officer, heretofore or hereafter promoted upon the retired list shall, in consequence of such promotion, be entitled to any increase of pay.

*　　　*　　　*　　　*　　　*　　　*

Approved July 15, 1870.

AN·ACT for the better government of the Navy of the United States.

*　　　*　　　*　　　*　　　*　　　*

SEC. 14. *And be it further enacted,* That in all cases where the crews of the ships or vessels of the United States shall be separated from their vessels, by the latter being wrecked, lost, or destroyed, all the command, power, and authority given to the officers of such ships or vessels shall remain and be in full force as effectually as if such ship or vessel were not so wrecked, lost, or destroyed, until such ship's company be regularly discharged from or ordered again into the service, or until a court-martial or court of inquiry shall be held to inquire into the loss of such ship or vessel; and if, by the sentence of such court, or other satisfactory evidence, it shall appear to the Secretary of the Navy that all or any of the officers and men of such ship's company did their utmost to preserve her, and after the loss thereof behaved themselves agreeably to the discipline of the Navy, then the pay and emoluments of such officers and men, or such of them as shall have done their duty, as aforesaid, shall go on until their discharge or death; and every officer or man who shall, after the loss of such vessel, act contrary to the discipline of the Navy, shall be punished, at the discretion of a court-martial, in the same manner as if such vessel had not been so lost. *[Authority of officers to continue over the crews of lost vessels. Pay and emoluments to continue to those who did their duty. Punishment for violating discipline of navy.]*

SEC. 15. *And be it further enacted,* That all the pay and emoluments of the officers and men of any of the ships or vessels of the United States taken by an enemy, who shall appear by the sentence of a court-martial, or otherwise, to have done their utmost to preserve and defend their ship or vessel, and after the taking thereof have behaved themselves obediently to their superiors, agreeably to the discipline of the Navy, shall go on, and be paid them until their death, exchange, or discharge. *[When vessels are taken by the enemy, pay and emoluments to continue to such as did their duty, &c.]*

*　　　*　　　*　　　*　　　*　　　*

Approved July 17, 1862.　(Vol. 12, p. 600.)

RATIONS.

AN ACT to establish and equalize the grades of line officers of the United States Navy.

*　　　*　　　*　　　*　　　*　　　*

SEC. 19. *And be it further enacted,* That all officers, while at sea or attached to a sea-going vessel, should be allowed one ration. *[Rations to officers.]*

*　　　*　　　*　　　*　　　*　　　*

Approved July 16, 1862.　(Vol. 12, p. 583.)

AN ACT making appropriations for the naval service for the year ending the thirtieth June, one thousand eight hundred and fifty-two.

To whom rations shall not be allowed.

Be it further enacted, That * * * no person not actually attached to, and doing duty on board a sea-going or receiving vessel, and the petty officers, seamen, and ordinary seamen attached to the ordinary of the navy yards,

Rations stopped for the sick.

shall be allowed a ration: *And provided further,* That no rations stopped for the sick on board vessels shall be credited to the hospital fund, but shall remain and be accounted for by the purser as a part of the provisions of the vessels, and that the rations of officers and others of the Navy, sent to hospitals on shore, shall be credited to the hospital fund at the cost only thereof.

* * * * * *

Approved March 3, 1851. (Vol. 9, p. 621.)

AN ACT making appropriations for the naval service for the year ending June thirtieth, eighteen hundred and seventy-one, and for other purposes.

* * * * * *

Commutation price of navy rations.

SEC. 4. * * * And from and after the thirtieth day of June, eighteen hundred and seventy, so much of the fourth section of the act * * * as allows to persons in the naval service five cents per day in lieu of the spirit ration, is hereby repealed, and from and after that day thirty cents shall in all cases be deemed the commutation price of the Navy ration.

* * * * * *

Approved July 15, 1870.

AN ACT to establish and equalize the grades of line officers of the United States Navy.

No rations to retired officers.

SEC. 20. * * * And no rations shall be allowed to any officers of the Navy on the retired list.

* * * * * *

Approved July 16, 1862. (Vol. 12, p. 583.)

MILEAGE.

AN ACT to regulate the pay of the Navy of the United States.

Mileage.

SEC. 2. * * * traveling expenses when under orders, for which ten cents per mile shall be allowed.

Approved March 3, 1835. (Vol. 4, p. 755.)

PRIZE AND BOUNTY.

AN ACT to regulate prize proceedings and the distribution of prize money, and for other purposes.

Decrees where the capturing vessel was of superior or equal force, or of inferior force.

SEC. 10. *And be it further enacted,* That the net proceeds of all property condemned as prize shall, when the prize was of superior or equal force to the vessel or vessels making the capture, be decreed to the captors; and when of inferior force, one-half shall be decreed to the United States and the other half to the captors: *Provided,* That in case of privateers and letters of marque, the whole shall be decreed to the captors, unless it shall be otherwise provided in the commissions issued to such vessels. All vessels of the Navy within signal distance of the vessel or vessels making the capture, under such circumstances and in such condition as to be able to render effective aid if required, shall share in the prize; and in case of vessels not of the Navy, none shall be entitled to share except the vessel or vessels making the capture, in which term shall be included vessels present at the capture and rendering actual assistance in the capture. All prize money adjudged to the captors shall be distributed in the following proportions, namely: Proviso—letters of marque. Vessels of navy within signal distance to share in the prize. Other vessels. Distribution of prize money.

First. To the commanding officer of a fleet or squadron, one-twentieth part of all prize money awarded to any vessel or vessels under his immediate command. To commanding officers of fleet or squadron.

Second. To the commanding officer of a division of a fleet or squadron, on duty under the orders of the commander-in-chief of such fleet or squadron, a sum equal to one-fiftieth part of any prize money awarded to a vessel of such division for a capture made while under his command, the said fiftieth part to be deducted from the moiety due to the United States, if there be such moiety, otherwise from the amount awarded to the captors: *Provided,* That such fiftieth part shall not be in addition to any share which may be due to the commander of the division, and which he may elect to receive, as commander of a single ship making or assisting in the capture. To commanding officer of a division.

Third. To the fleet captain, one-hundredth part of all prize money awarded to any vessel or vessels of the fleet or squadron in which he is serving, except in a case where the capture is made by the vessel on board of which he is serving at the time of such capture; and in such case he shall share, in proportion to his pay, with the other officers and men on board such vessel, as is hereinafter provided. To fleet captain.

Fourth. To the commander of a single ship, one-tenth part of all the prize money awarded to the ship under his command, if such ship at the time of the capture was under the command of the commanding officer of a fleet or squadron, or a division, and three-twentieths if his ship was acting independently of such superior officer. To commander of a single ship.

Fifth. After the foregoing deductions, the residue shall be distributed and proportioned among all others doing duty on board, (including the fleet captain,) and borne upon the books of the ship, in proportion to their respective rates of pay in the service. To all others doing duty on board, &c.

*　　*　　*　　*　　*　　*

SEC. 11. *And be it further enacted,* That a bounty shall be paid by the United States for each person on board any ship or vessel of war belonging to an enemy at the commencement of an engagement, which shall be sunk or otherwise destroyed in such engagement by any ship or vessel belonging to the United States, or which it may be necessary to destroy in consequence of injuries sustained in action, of Bounty for destruction of vessels of war belonging to the enemy.

one hundred dollars if the enemy's vessel was of inferior force, and of two hundred dollars if of equal or superior force, to be divided among the officers and crew in the same manner as prize money; and when the actual number of men on board any such vessel cannot be satisfactorily ascertained, it shall be estimated according to the complement allowed to vessels of its class in the Navy of the United States; and there shall be paid as bounty to the captors of any vessel of war captured from an enemy, which they may be instructed to destroy, or which shall be immediately destroyed for the public interest, but not in consequence of injuries received in action, fifty dollars for every person who shall be on board at the time of such capture. All ransom money, salvage, bounty, or proceeds of condemned property, accruing or awarded to any vessel of the Navy, shall be distributed and paid to the officers and men entitled thereto in the same manner as prize money, under the direction of the Secretary of the Navy.

Bounty for vessels of war captured from t h e enemy, &c.

Ransom money, salvage, &c., to be distributed as prize money.

* * * * * *

Approved June 30, 1864. (Vol. 13, p. 306.)

AN ACT making appropriations for the support of the Army for the year ending June thirty, eighteen hundred and seventy-one, and for other purposes.

* * * * * *

Land-bounty of one quarter-section.

SEC. 25. *And be it further enacted*, That * * * every seaman, marine, and officer, or other person, who has served in the Navy of the United States, or in the Marine Corps or Revenue Marine, during the rebellion, for ninety days, and remained loyal to the Government, shall, on payment of the fee or commission to any register or receiver of any land office required by law, be entitled to enter one quarter-section of land, not mineral, of the alternate reserved sections of public lands along the lines of any one of the railroads or other public works in the United States, wherever public lands have been or may be granted by acts of Congress, and to receive a patent therefor under and by virtue of the provisions of the act to secure homesteads to actual settlers on the public domain, and the acts amendatory thereof, and on the terms and conditions therein prescribed; and all the provisions of said acts, except as herein modified, shall extend and be applicable to entries under this act, and the Commissioner of the General Land Office is hereby authorized to prescribe the necessary rules and regulations to carry this section into effect, and determine all facts necessary therefor.

Approved July 15, 1870.

COMPENSATION AND RELIEF.

AN ACT for the relief of seamen and others borne on the books of vessels wrecked or lost in the naval service.

*   *   *   *   *   *

SEC. 2. *And be it further enacted,* That the proper accounting officers of the Treasury be, and they are hereby, authorized, in settling the accounts of the petty officers, seamen, and others, not officers, on board of any vessel in the employ of the United States which, by any casualty, or in action with the enemy, has been or may be sunk or otherwise destroyed, *   *   * to allow and pay to each person, not an officer, employed on a vessel so sunk or otherwise destroyed, and whose personal effects have been lost, a sum not exceeding sixty dollars as compensation for loss of his personal effects. *(Last quarterly return of paymaster to be assumed as a basis for computation in certain cases. Compensation for loss of personal effects.)*

SEC. 3. *And be it further enacted,* That in case of the death of such petty officer, seaman, or other person, not an officer, such payment shall be made to the widow, child, or children, father, mother, brothers, and sisters, (jointly,) in that order of preference, under such rules as the Second Comptroller of the Treasury may prescribe; such credits and gratuity to be paid out of any money in the Treasury not otherwise appropriated. *(How payments are to be made in case of the death of petty officers, &c.)*

Approved July 4, 1864.   (Vol. 13, p. 389.)

AN ACT to amend an act entitled "An act for the relief of seamen and others borne on the books of vessels wrecked or lost in the naval service," approved July four, eighteen hundred and sixty-four, and for other purposes.

Be it enacted by the Senate and House of Representatives of the United States of America in Congress assembled, That in case any officer of the Navy or Marine Corps on board a vessel in the employ of the United States which, by any casualty, or in action with the enemy, has been or may be sunk or otherwise destroyed, shall thereby have lost his personal effects, the proper accounting officers are hereby authorized, with the approval of the Secretary of the Navy, to allow such officer a sum not exceeding the amount of his sea-pay for one month, as compensation for such loss: *Provided,* That such loss has not occurred through the negligence or want of skill or foresight of the officer making application for such loss: *Provided,* That the accounting officers shall, in all cases, require a schedule and certificate from the officer making the claim for effects so lost: *And provided further,* That no allowance shall be made by virtue of this act for any loss incurred prior to the nineteenth day of April, eighteen hundred and sixty-one. *(Compensation to officers for loss of personal effects. Provisos.)*

*   *   *   *   *   *

Approved April 6, 1866.

PENSIONS.

AN ACT for the better government of the Navy of the United States.

* * * * * *

Pensions for disability.

SEC. 13. *And be it further enacted*, That every officer, seaman, or marine, disabled in the line of his duty, shall be entitled to receive for life, or during his disability, a pension from the United States, according to the nature and degree of his disability, not exceeding in any case his monthly pay.

* * * * * *

Approved July 17, 1862. (Vol. 12, p. 600.)

Extract from an act renewing certain naval pensions and extending the benefits of existing laws, respecting naval pensions to engineers, firemen, and coal-heavers in the Navy, and to their widows.

Pension benefits extended to persons in the Engineer Department.

SEC. 2. That engineers, firemen, and coal-heavers in the Navy shall be entitled to pensions in the same manner as officers, seamen, and marines, and the widows of engineers, firemen, and coal-heavers in the same manner as the widows of officers, seamen, and marines. * * * * *

* * * * * *

Approved August 11, 1848.

AN ACT to grant pensions.

Be it enacted by the Senate and House of Representatives of the United States of America in Congress assembled, That if any officer, non-commissioned officer, musician, or private of the Army, including regulars, volunteers, and militia, or any officer, warrant or petty officer, musician, seaman, ordinary seaman, flotilla-man, marine, clerk, landsman, pilot, or other person in the Navy or Marine Corps, has been, since the fourth day of March, eighteen hundred and sixty-one, or shall hereafter be, disabled by reason of any wound received or disease contracted while in the service of the United States, and in the line of duty, he shall, upon making due proof of the fact according to such forms and regulations as are or may be provided by or in pursuance of law, be placed upon the list of invalid pensions of the United States, and be entitled to receive, for the highest rate of disability, such pension as is hereinafter provided in such cases, and for an inferior disability an amount proportionate to the highest disability, to commence as hereinafter provided, and continue during the existence of such disability. The pension for a total disability for officers, non-commissioned officers, musicians, and privates employed in the military service of the United States, whether regulars, volunteers, or militia, and in the Marine Corps, shall be as follows, viz: Lieutenant colonel, and all officers of a higher rank, thirty dollars per month; major, twenty-five dollars per month; captain, twenty dollars per month; first lieutenant, seventeen dollars per month; second lieutenant, fifteen dollars; and non-commissioned officers, musicians, and privates, eight dollars per month. The pension for total disability for officers, warrant or petty officers, and others employed in the naval service of the United States, shall be as follows, viz: Captain, commander, surgeon, paymaster, and chief engineer, respectively, ranking with commander by law, lieutenant commanding, and master commanding, thirty dollars per month; lieutenant, surgeon, paymaster, and chief engineer, respectively, ranking with lieutenant by law, and passed assistant surgeon, twenty-five dollars per month; professor of mathematics, master, assistant surgeon, assistant paymaster, and chaplain, twenty dollars per month; first assistant engineers and pilots, fifteen dollars per month; passed midshipman, midshipman, captain's and paymaster's clerk, second and third assistant engineer, master's mate, and all warrant officers, ten dollars per month; all petty officers, and all other persons before named employed in the naval service, eight dollars per month; and all commissioned officers of either service shall receive such and only such pension as is herein provided for the rank in which they hold commissions. *(For total disability. Of chief engineer. Of chief engineer. Of first assistant engineer. Of second and third assistant engineers, petty officers and all other persons.)*

SEC. 2. *And be it further enacted*, That if any officer or other person named in the first section of this act has died since the fourth day of March, eighteen hundred and sixty-one, or shall hereafter die, by reason of any wound received or disease contracted while in the service of the United States, and in the line of duty, his widow, or if there be no widow, his child or children under sixteen years of age, shall be entitled to receive the same pension as the husband or father would have been entitled to had he been totally disabled, to commence from the death of the husband or father, and to continue to the widow during her widowhood, or to the child or children until they severally attain to the age of sixteen years, and no longer. *(Their widows or children, under sixteen years of age to receive the same pension after the death of the husband or father.)*

SEC. 3. *And be it further enacted*, That where any officer, or other person named in the first section of this act, shall have died subsequently to the fourth day of March, eighteen hundred and sixty-one, or shall hereafter die, by reason of any wound received or disease contracted while in the service of the United States, and in the line of duty, and has not left or shall not leave a widow nor legitimate child, but has left or shall leave a mother who was dependent upon him for support, in whole or in part, the mother shall be entitled to receive the same pension as such officer or other person would have been entitled to had he been totally disabled; which pension shall commence from the death of the officer or other person dying as aforesaid: *Provided, however*, That if such mother herself shall be in receipt of a pension as a widow, in virtue of the provisions of the second section of this act, in that case no pension or allowance shall be granted to her on account of her son, unless she gives up the other pension or allowance: *And provided, further*, That the pension given to a mother on account of her son shall terminate on her re-marriage: *And provided, further*, That nothing herein shall be so construed as to *(A mother—when to receive the pension.)*

entitle the mother of an officer or other person dying, as aforesaid, to more than one pension at the same time under the provisions of this act.

SEC. 4. *And be it further enacted*, That where any officer or other person named in the first section of this act shall have died subsequently to the fourth day of March, eighteen hundred and sixty-one, or shall hereafter die, by reason of any wound received or disease contracted while in the service of the United States, and in the line of duty, and has not left or shall not leave a widow, nor legitimate child, nor mother, but has left or may leave an orphan sister or sisters under sixteen years of age, who were dependent upon him for support, in whole or in part, such sister or sisters shall be entitled to receive the same pension as such officer or other person would have been entitled to had he been totally disabled; which pension to said orphan shall commence from the death of the officer or other person dying as aforesaid, and shall continue to the said orphans until they severally arrive at the age of sixteen years, and no longer: *Provided, however*, That nothing herein shall be so construed as to entitle said orphans to more than one pension at the same time, under the provisions of this act: *And provided, further*, That no moneys shall be paid to the widow, or children, or any heirs of any deceased soldier on account of bounty, back pay, or pension, who have in any way been engaged in or who have aided or abetted the existing rebellion in the United States; but the right of such disloyal widow or children, heir or heirs of such soldier, shall be vested in the loyal heir or heirs of the deceased, if any there be.

SEC. 5. *And be it further enacted*, That pensions which may be granted, in pursuance of the provisions of this act, to persons who may have been, or shall be, employed in the military or naval service of the United States, shall commence on the day of the discharge of such persons in all cases in which the application for such provisions [pensions] is filed within one year after the date of said discharge; and in cases in which the application is not filed during said year, pensions granted to persons employed as aforesaid shall commence on the day of the filing of the application.

*   *   *   *   *   *

SEC. 9. *And be it further enacted*, That the Commissioner of Pensions, on application made to him in person or by letter by any claimants or applicants for pension, bounty, or other allowance required by law to be adjusted and paid by the Pension Office, shall furnish such claimants, free of all expense or charge to them, all such printed instructions and forms as may be necessary in establishing and obtaining said claim; and in case such claim is prosecuted by an agent or attorney of such claimant or applicant, on the issue of a certificate of pension or the granting of a bounty or allowance, the Commissioner of Pensions shall forthwith notify the applicant or claimant that such certificate has been issued or allowance made, and the amount thereof.

*   *   *   *   *   *

Approved July 14, 1862.

AN ACT relating to pensions.

Be it enacted by the Senate and House of Representatives of the United States of America in Congress assembled, That the laws granting pensions to the hereinafter-mentioned relatives of deceased persons leaving neither widow nor child entitled to pensions under existing laws, shall be so construed as to give precedence to such relatives in the following order, namely: First, mothers; secondly, fathers; thirdly, orphan brothers and sisters under sixteen years of age, who shall be pensioned jointly if there be more than one. * * *   [Order of precedence of relatives.]

SEC. 2. *And be it further enacted,* That no person shall be entitled to a pension by reason of wounds received or disease contracted in the service of the United States subsequently to the passage of this act unless the person who was wounded or contracted disease was in the line of duty; and * * * if in the naval service, was at the time borne on the books of some ship, or other vessel of the United States, at sea or in harbor, actually in commission, or was on his way, by direction of competent authority, to the United States, or to some other vessel or naval station.   [Disability must have taken place in the line of duty.]

SEC. 3. * * * the failure of any pensioner to claim his or her pension for a period of three years after the same shall have become due shall be deemed presumptive evidence that such pension has legally terminated by reason of the pensioner's death, remarriage, recovery from disability, or otherwise, and the pensioner's name shall be stricken from the rolls, subject to the right of restoration to the same on a new application, with evidence satisfactorily accounting for the failure to claim such pension.   [If a pension is not claimed for three years the pensioner's name to be stricken from the rolls, subject, &c.]

SEC. 4. *And be it further enacted,* That if any officer, soldier, seaman, or enlisted man has died since the fourth day of March, eighteen hundred and sixty-one, or shall hereafter die, leaving a widow entitled to a pension, and a child or children under sixteen years of age by a former wife, each of said children shall be entitled to receive two dollars per month, to commence from the death of their father and continue until they severally attain the age of sixteen years, to be paid to the guardian of such child or children for their use and benefit: *Provided, however,* That in all cases where such widow is charged with the care, custody, and maintenance of such child or children, the said sum of two dollars per month for each of said children shall be paid to her for and during the time she is, or may have been, so charged with the care, custody, and maintenance of such child or children, subject to the same conditions, provisions, and limitations as if they were her own children by her said deceased husband.   [Allowance to each child under sixteen years of age.] [Proviso.]

SEC. 5. *And be it further enacted,* That in all cases where an increased pension has been or may hereafter be granted to any widow or guardian of the children under sixteen years of age of a deceased soldier or sailor, * * * such widow, or the guardian of such children, shall not be deprived of such increase by reason of any child or children of such deceased soldier or sailor being the inmate of any home, orphan's asylum, or other public or private charitable   [Children not to be disallowed though they may be in a charitable institution.]

4 E C

institution organized for the care and education of soldiers' orphans under the laws of any of the States, or in any school or institution where such orphan may in whole or in part be maintained or educated at the expense of a State or of the public.

Pensions granted as specified herein, when to commence.

SEC. 6. *And be it further enacted*, That all pensions which have been granted in consequence of death occurring or disease contracted or wounds received since the fourth day of March, eighteen hundred and sixty-one, or which may hereafter be granted, shall commence from the discharge or from the death of the person on whose account the pension has been or shall hereafter be granted: *Provided*, That the

Proviso.

application for such pension has been or shall hereafter be filed with the Commissioner of Pensions within five years after the right thereto shall have accrued; except that applications by or in behalf of insane persons and children under sixteen years of age may be filed after the expiration of the said five years, if previously thereto they were without guardians or other proper legal representatives.

*   *   *   *   *

A widow may be deprived of her pension, which may be paid to the guardian of her children.

SEC. 8. *And be it further enacted*, * * * * That if any officer, soldier, or seaman shall have died of wounds received or of disease contracted in the line of duty in the military or naval service of the United States, leaving a widow and a child or children under the age of sixteen years, and it shall be duly certified, under seal, by any court having probate jurisdiction, that satisfactory evidence has been produced before such court that the widow aforesaid has abandoned the care of such child or children, or is an unsuitable person, by reason of immoral conduct, to have the custody of the same, or on presentation of satisfactory evidence thereof to the Commissioner of Pensions, then no pension shall be allowed to such widow until said child or children shall have severally become sixteen years of age, any previous enactment to the contrary notwithstanding; and the child or children aforesaid shall be pensioned in the same manner as if no widow had survived the said officer, soldier, or seaman, and such pension may be paid to the regularly authorized guardian of such child or children.

Certain pensions may be paid to the heirs or representatives.

SEC. 9. *And be it further enacted*, * * * * That if any person entitled to a pension has died since March four, eighteen hundred and sixty-one, or shall hereafter die while an application for such pension is pending, leaving no widow and no child under sixteen years of age, his or her heirs or legal representatives shall be entitled to receive the accrued pension to which the applicant would have been entitled had the certificate been issued before his or her death.

*   *   *   *   *   *

Approved July 27, 1868.

AN ACT supplementary to the several acts relating to pensions.

Be it enacted, &c., * * * That from and after the passage of this act, all persons by law entitled to a less pension than hereinafter specified, who, while in the military or naval service, and in line of duty, shall have lost the sight of both eyes, or who shall have lost both hands, or been permanently and totally disabled in the same or otherwise so permanently and totally disabled as to render them utterly helpless, or so nearly so as to require the constant personal aid and attendance of another person, shall be entitled to a pension of twenty-five dollars a month; and all persons who, under like circumstances, shall have lost both feet, or one hand and one foot, or been totally and permanently disabled in the same, or otherwise so disabled as to be incapacitated for performing any manual labor, but not so much so as to require constant personal aid and attention, shall be entitled to a pension of twenty dollars per month; and all persons who, under like circumstances, shall have lost one hand or one foot, or been totally and permanently disabled in the same, or otherwise so disabled as to render their inability to perform manual labor equivalent to the loss of a hand or foot, shall be entitled to a pension of fifteen dollars per month.

Pension to the totally blind or disabled requiring constant personal attendance.

To the totally disabled who do not require constant attendance.

Pension to those who have lost one hand or one foot.

*   *   *   *   *   *

Approved June 6, 1866.

AN ACT relating to pensions.

*   *   *   *   *   *

SEC. 12. *And be it further enacted*, That section   *   * shall be so construed as to secure to every person entitled by law *   *   *   * to a less pension than twenty-five dollars per month, who, while in the military or naval service and in the line of duty, or in consequence of wounds received or disease contracted therein, having only one eye, shall have lost the same, a pension of twenty-five dollars per month.

Pensions to the totally blind.

*   *   *   *   *   *

Approved July 27, 1868.

AN ACT making appropriations for the payment of revolutionary and other pensioners of the United States for the fiscal year ending on the thirtieth of June, one thousand eight hundred and forty-five.

Be it enacted, &c., *   *   * *Provided*, That no pension shall be hereafter granted to a widow for the same time that her husband received one: *And provided, also,* That no person in the Army, Navy, or Marine Corps shall be allowed to draw both a pension as an invalid and the pay of his rank or station in the service, unless the alleged disability for which the pension was granted be such as to have occasioned his employment in a lower grade, or in some civil branch of the service.*

No pension to a widow for a time her husband received one.

Pension and pay not to be drawn at same time, except, &c.

Approved April 30, 1844.   (Vol. 5, p. 656.)

------

* Not to be construed so as to exclude officers, seamen, or marines from their pensions when disabled for sea-service: *Provided*, That the whole amount received by the pensioner, including pay for his service and pensions, shall not exceed his lowest duty-pay. (Act of August 11, 1848.)

AN ACT supplementary to the several acts relating to pensions.

*   *   *   *   *   *

Only one pension to be received at the same time.

SEC. 13. *And be it further enacted*, That nothing in this or any other act shall be so construed as to   *   *   *   * entitle a person to receive more than one pension at the same time, and in every case in which a claim for pension

Pension on a delayed claim— when to commence.

shall not have been filed within three years after the discharge or decease of the party on whose account the claim is made, the pension, if allowed, shall commence from the date of filing the last paper in said case by the party prosecuting the same.

*   *   *   *   *   *

Approved June 6, 1866.

––––––

AN ACT to construe certain acts therein cited in relation to pensions.

Pensions by special acts not changed.

Be it enacted by the Senate and House of Representatives of the United States of America in Congress assembled, That neither the act of July twenty-fifth, eighteen hundred and sixty-six, entitled "An act increasing the pensions of widows and orphans, and for other purposes," nor the act of July twenty-seventh, eighteen hundred and sixty-eight, entitled "An act relating to pensions," shall be so construed as to increase the amount directed to be paid in any special act of Congress granting a pension ; nor shall said acts be construed so as to reduce the same, whenever such act fixes definitely the amount of pension to which the person therein named shall be entitled, in excess of the rate fixed by general law for the rank in respect to which such special pensions may have been or may hereafter be granted.   *   *   *

Approved July 7, 1870.

––––––

ARTIFICIAL LIMBS.

AN ACT supplementary to "An act to provide for furnishing artificial limbs to disabled soldiers."

Rights to artificial limbs, &c., extended to persons in the navy.

Be it enacted by the Senate and House of Representatives of the United States of America in Congress assembled, That the benefits of the act approved June seventeenth, eighteen hundred and seventy, entitled "An act to provide for furnishing artificial limbs to disabled soldiers," shall be extended to all officers, soldiers, seamen, and marines disabled in the military or naval service of the United States as fully as the same are provided for in the acts approved July sixteenth, eighteen hundred and sixty-two, July twenty-eighth, eighteen hundred and sixty-six, and July twenty-seventh, eighteen hundred and sixty-eight, in so far as the said acts relate to artificial limbs and to transportation for procuring said limbs.

Approved June 30, 1870.

[Extract from the act referred to in the foregoing act.]

AN ACT to provide for furnishing artificial limbs to disabled soldiers.

Be it enacted by the Senate and House of Representatives of the United States of America in Congress assembled, That every soldier who was disabled during the late war for the suppression of the rebellion, and who was furnished by the War Department with an artificial limb, or apparatus for resection, shall be entitled to receive a new limb or apparatus as soon after the passage of this act as the same can be *practically* [practicably] furnished, and at the expiration of every five years thereafter, under such regulations as may be prescribed by the Surgeon General of the Army: *Provided,* That the soldier may, if he so elect, receive, instead of said limb or apparatus, the money value thereof, at the following rates, viz: For artificial legs, seventy-five dollars; for arms, fifty dollars; for feet, fifty dollars; for apparatus for resection, fifty dollars. *The money value of the limbs may be received.*

*   *   *   *   *   *

SEC. 3. *And be it further enacted,* That every soldier who lost a limb during the late war, but from the nature of his injury was not able to use an artificial limb, and consequently received none from the Government, shall be entitled to the benefits of this act and shall receive money commutation as hereinbefore provided. *Commutation when an artificial limb cannot be used.*

Approved June 17, 1870.

GENERAL ORDER.

NAVY DEPARTMENT,
March 2, 1861.

Whenever any officer of the corps of surgeons, paymaster, or engineers is arraigned for trial before a court of inquiry or court-martial, the court shall consist, in part, of officers of the corps to which the accused belongs. *Courts to try a staff officer to consist in part of officers of his corps.*

ISAAC TOUCEY,
Secretary of the Navy.

THE RIGHT OF SUFFRAGE.

AN ACT to prevent officers of the Army and Navy, and other persons engaged in the military and naval service of the United States, from interfering in elections in the States.

Be it enacted &c., *   *   * *Provided,* That nothing herein contained shall be so construed as to prevent any officers, soldiers, sailors, or marines from exercising the right of suffrage in any election district to which he may belong, if otherwise qualified, according to the laws of the State in which he shall offer to vote. *Officers, soldiers, sailors, or marines may exercise the right of suffrage.*

*   *   *   *   *   *

Approved February 25, 1865.   (Vol. 13, p. 437.)

BRIBERY.

AN ACT to prevent members of Congress and officers of the Government of the United States from taking consideration for procuring contracts, office, or place from the United States, and for other purposes.

Members of Congress and Government officers not to receive a consideration for procuring contracts, &c·

Be it enacted by the Senate and House of Representatives of the United States of America in Congress assembled, That * * * any officer* of the Government of the United States who shall, directly or indirectly, take, receive, or agree to receive, any money, property, or other valuable consideration whatsoever, from any person or persons for procuring, or aiding to procure, any contract, office, or place from the Government of the United States or any department thereof, or from any officer of the United States, for any person or persons whatsoever, or for giving any such contract, office, or place to any person whomsoever, and the person or per-

Persons forbidden to offer such considerations.

sons who shall directly or indirectly offer or agree to give, or give, or bestow, any money, property, or other valuable consideration whatsoever, for the procuring or aiding to procure any contract, office, or place, as aforesaid, * * * shall, for every such offense, be liable to indictment as for a misdemeanor in any court of the United States having jurisdiction thereof, and on conviction thereof shall pay a fine of

Fine and imprisonment on conviction thereof.

not exceeding ten thousand dollars, and suffer imprisonment in the penitentiary not exceeding two years, at the discretion of the court trying the same; and any such contract or agreement, as aforesaid, may, at the option of the President

Contract may be declared null and void.

of the United States, be absolutely null and void; and any * * * officer of the United States convicted, as afore-

Disqualification for office.

said, shall, moreover, be disqualified from holding any office of honor, profit, or trust under the Government of the United States.

Approved July 16, 1862. (Vol. 12, p. 577.)

HOSPITAL FUND, MEDICINES, &c.

AN ACT in addition to "An act for the relief of sick and disabled seamen."

* * * * * *

Twenty cents a month to be deducted from pay of the Navy.

SEC. 2. * * * The Secretary of the Navy shall be, and he hereby is, authorized and directed to deduct, after the first day of September next, from the pay thereafter to become due, of the officers, seamen, and marines of the Navy of the United States, at the rate of twenty cents per month, for every such officer, seamen, and marine,†‡

* * * * * *

---

* The provisions of this act shall be so construed as to embrace any agent of the Government of the United States.—(Act of February 25, 1863, vol. 12, p. 696.)

† "Each officer, warrant officer, petty officer, seaman, ordinary seaman, fireman, and coal-heaver, in the Navy." (Statutes relative to the United States Navy, 1869, pp. 42 and 43.)

‡ By the 11th section of the act for the better government of the Navy, approved July 17, 1862, all money accruing or already accrued

to be applied to the same purposes as the money collected
by virtue of the above mentioned act is appropriated.

*　　　*　　　*　　　*　　　*　　　*

Approved March 2, 1799. (Statutes at Large, vol. 1, p.
729.)

AN ACT establishing Navy hospitals.

*　　　*　　　*　　　*　　　*　　　*

SEC. 2. That all fines imposed on Navy officers, seamen, *Fines imposed to go to Navy hospitals.*
and marines, shall be paid to * 　* Navy hospitals.

*　　　*　　　*　　　*　　　*　　　*

SEC. 5. That, when any Navy officer, seaman, or marine *Disposition of rations and pensions to those admitted into the hospitals.*
shall be admitted into a Navy hospital, the institution shall
be allowed one ration per day during his continuance
therein, to be deducted from the account of the United
States with such officer, seaman, or marine; and in like
manner, when any officer, seaman, or marine entitled to a
pension shall be admitted into a Navy hospital, such pension, during his continuance therein, shall be paid to * *
Navy hospitals, and deducted from the account of such pensioner.

Approved February 26, 1811.   (Vol. 2, p. 650.)

That the rations of persons in the Navy sent to hospitals
on shore shall be credited to the hospital fund. (See p. 42.)

AN ACT making appropriations for the naval service for the year ending June thirtieth, eighteen hundred and seventy-one, and for other
purposes.

*　　　*　　　*　　　*　　　*　　　*

SEC. 17. *And be it further enacted*, That expenses incurred *Expenses for medicines and medical attendance when off duty.*
by any officer of the Navy for medicines and medical at-
tendance shall not be allowed unless they were incurred
when he was on duty, and the medicines could not have
been obtained from naval supplies, or the attendance of a
naval medical officer could not have been had.

*　　　*　　　*　　　*　　　*　　　*

Approved July 15, 1870.

---

to the United States from the sale of prizes is to remain forever a fund
for the payment of pensions to the officers, seamen, and marines who
may be entitled to receive the same; and by resolution of July 1, 1864,
the Secretary of the Navy, as trustee of the naval pension fund, is
authorized and directed to invest it in registered securities of the
United States, &c.

HOSPITAL FOR THE INSANE.

AN ACT to organize an institution for the insane of the Army and Navy, and of the District of Columbia, in the said District.

Objects of the Hospital for the Insane. *Be it enacted,* That the title of the institution shall be the Government Hospital for the Insane, and its object shall be the most humane care and enlightened curative treatment of the insane of the Army and Navy of the United States, and of the District of Columbia.

*　　　*　　　*　　　*　　　*　　　*

Approved March 3, 1855.　(Vol. 10, p. 682.)

———

AN ACT to amend an act entitled "An act to organize an institution for the insane of the Army and Navy, and of the District of Columbia, in the said District."

*　　　*　　　*　　　*　　　*　　　*

Admission of insane of Navy, &c., into Government asylum. SEC. 4. *And be it further enacted,* That the order of the Secretary of War, and that of the Secretary of the Navy, and that of the Secretary of the Treasury, shall authorize the superintendent to receive insane persons belonging to the Army and Navy and revenue-cutter service, respectively, and keep them in custody until they are cured or removed by the same authority which ordered their reception.

Approved June 1, 1860.　(Vol. 12, p. 23.)

———

AN ACT making appropriations for sundry civil expenses of the Government for the year ending the thirtieth of June, eighteen hundred and sixty-five, and for other purposes.

Government Hospital for the Insane. *Be it enacted by the Senate and House of Representatives of the United States of America in Congress assembled,*

*　　　*　　　*　　　*　　　*　　　*

That the Secretary of the Navy is hereby authorized and required to set apart from the pay of any officer of the Navy, or of the Marine Corps, who may be under treatment by his order in the Government Hospital for the Insane, *Portion of pay of inmates to be set aside for their comfort.* such a portion of the monthly pay of said officer as may be needed for his personal use and comfort in addition to the ordinary resources of that establishment.

*　　　*　　　*　　　*　　　*　　　*

Approved July 2, 1864.　(Vol. 13, p. 344.)

———

FURLOUGH AND SICK LEAVE.

AN ACT to increase and regulate the pay of the Navy of the United States.

*　　　*　　　*　　　*　　　*　　　*

Right to furlough officers. SEC. 4. *And be it further enacted,* That nothing in this act contained shall be held to modify or affect the existing power of the Secretary of the Navy to furlough officers or to affect the furlough pay.

*　　　*　　　*　　　*　　　*　　　*

Approved June 1, 1860.　(Vol. 12, p. 23.)

For furlough pay, see page 40.

AN ACT supplementary to the several acts relating to pensions.

*   *   *   *   *   *

SEC. 8. *And be it further enacted,* That officers absent on sick leave, and enlisted men absent on sick furlough, shall be regarded in the administration of the pension laws in the same manner as if they were in the field or hospital.

In the matter of pension, sick leave or furlough to be considered as sickness on active duty.

*   *   *   *   *   *

Approved June 6, 1866.

RESERVED AND RETIRED OFFICERS.

AN ACT to further promote the efficiency of the Navy.

Be it enacted by the Senate and House of Representatives of the United States of America in Congress assembled, That whenever the name of any naval officer* now in the service, or who may hereafter be in the service of the United States, shall have been born on the Naval Register forty-five years, or shall be of the age of sixty-two years, he shall be retired from active service, and his name entered on the retired list of officers of the grade to which he belonged at the time of such retirement.†

Officers borne on the register 45 years. or 62 years of age, to be retired.

SEC. 2. *And be it further enacted,* That the President of the United States be, and he is hereby, authorized to assign any officer who may be retired under the preceding section of this act to shore duty; and such officer thus assigned shall receive the full shore pay of his grade while so employed.

President may assign retired officers to shore duty.

*   *   *   *   *   *

Approved December 21, 1861.   (Vol. 12, p. 329.)

AN ACT providing for the better organization of the military establishment.

*   *   *   *   *   *

SEC. 22. *And be it further enacted,* That if any officer of the Navy shall have become, or shall hereafter become, incapable of performing the duties of his office, he shall be placed upon the retired list and withdrawn from active service and command and from the line of promotion.

Retirement of incapable officers.

*   *   *   *   *   *

The next officer in rank shall be promoted to the place of the retired officer, according to the established rules of the service. And the same rule of promotion shall be applied successively to the vacancies consequent upon the retirement of an officer.

Promotions to vacancies caused thereby.

SEC. 23. *And be it further enacted,* That whenever any officer of the Navy, on being ordered to perform the duties appropriate to his commission, shall report himself unable to comply with such order, or whenever, in the judgment of the President of the United States, an officer of the Navy shall be in any way incapacitated from performing the

Board to decide the incapacity of Navy officers.

duties of his office, the President, at his discretion, shall direct the Secretary of the Navy to refer the case of such officer to a board of not more than nine, and not less than five, commissioned officers, two-fifths of whom shall be members of the medical bureau of the Navy; the board, *How composed; duty.* except those taken from the medical bureau, to be composed, if possible, (as far as may be,) of his seniors in rank. The determination of the board in each case shall, with a record of its proceedings, be transmitted to the Secretary of the Navy, to be laid before the President for his approval or disapproval, and orders in the case. The board, whenever it *Report.* finds an officer incapacitated for active service, will report whether, in its judgment, the incapacity result from long and faithful service, from wounds or injury received in the line of duty, from sickness or exposure therein, or from any other incident of service; if so, and the President approve *Effect of decision when approved.* of such judgment, the disabled officer shall thereupon be placed upon the list of retired officers, according to the provisions of this act. But if such disability or incompetency proceeded from other causes, and the President concur in opinion with the board, the officer may be retired upon furlough pay, or he shall be wholly retired from the service, with one year's pay, at the discretion of the President; and in this last case his name shall be wholly omitted from the Navy Register. The members of the board shall, in every *Members to be sworn.* case, be sworn to an honest and impartial discharge of their duties, and no officer of the Navy shall be retired, either partially or wholly, from the service without having had a *Officers may be heard.* fair and full hearing before the board, if he shall demand it.

SEC. 24. *And be it further enacted,* That the retired officers *Privileges and liabilities of retired officers.* shall be entitled to wear the uniform of their respective grades, shall continue to be borne upon the Navy Register, shall be subject to the rules and articles governing the Navy, and to trial by general court-martial.

*   *   *   *   *   *

Approved August 3, 1861. (Vol. 12, p. 287.)

AN ACT to amend certain acts in relation to the Navy.

*   *   *   *   *   *

Retired and reserved officers entitled to promotion. SEC. 9. *And be it further enacted,* That officers on the retired and reserved lists of the Navy shall be entitled to promotion as their several dates upon the active list are *But not to pay beyond, &c.* promoted; but such promotion shall not entitle them to any pay beyond that to which they were entitled when retired, *To receive full pay upon active duty.* unless upon active duty, when they shall receive the full pay of their respective grades. * * * *

Approved March 2, 1867.

For the pay of retired officers not on active duty, see p. 40.

That no ration is granted to retired officers, see p. 42.

AN ACT making appropriations for the naval service for the year ending June thirtieth, eighteen hundred and seventy-one, and for other purposes.

*   *   *   *   *   *

SEC. 6. *And be it further enacted,* That no officer of the Navy shall, because of misconduct, be placed on the retired list; but he shall be brought to trial by court-martial for such misconduct; nor shall any lieutenant commander, lieutenant, master, ensign, midshipman, passed assistant surgeon, passed assistant paymaster, first assistant engineer, assistant surgeon, assistant paymaster, or second assistant engineer be placed on the retired list, except on account of physical or mental disability. *(No officer to be retired for misconduct. Junior officers to be retired only for disability.)*

*   *   *   *   *   *

Approved July 15, 1870.

AN ACT making appropriations for the naval service for the year ending June thirty, eighteen hundred and seventy-two, and for other purposes.

*   *   *   *   *   *

SEC. 11. That officers of the medical, pay, and engineer corps, chaplains and professors of mathematics, and also constructors, who shall have served faithfully for forty-five years, shall, when retired, have the relative rank of commodore; and officers of these several corps who have been or shall be retired at the age of sixty-two years, before having served for forty-five years, but who shall have served faithfully until retired, on the completion of forty years from their entry into the service, shall also from that time have the relative rank of commodore; and staff officers who have been or shall be retired for causes incident to the service before arriving at sixty-two years of age shall have the same rank on the retired list as pertained to their position on the active list: *Provided, however,* That nothing contained in this section shall be construed to increase the pay now provided for said several staff officers. *(Rank of staff officers retired for length of service or age.)*

SEC. 12. *   *   *   Officers of the staff now on the retired list shall have the rank thereon to which they would have been entitled had they remained on the active list, unless they shall be entitled to higher rank. *   *   *   *

Approved March 3, 1871.

DISMISSAL.

AN ACT making appropriations for the support of the Army for the year ending thirtieth of June, eighteen hundred and sixty-seven, and for other purposes.

*   *   *   *   *   *

SEC. 5. *   *   *   And no officer in the *   *   naval service, shall, in time of peace, be dismissed from the service except upon and in pursuance of the sentence of a court-martial to that effect, or in commutation thereof. *(Dismissal only in pursuance of sentence of court-martial, &c.)*

*   *   *   *   *   *

Approved July 13, 1866.

AN ACT to establish and equalize the grades of line officers of the
United States Navy.

* * * * * *

A dismissed officer disqualified from again becoming an officer. .
Nor shall any officer of the Navy who has been dismissed
by sentence of a court-martial, or suffered to resign to
escape one, ever again become an officer of the Navy.

* * * * * *

Approved July 16, 1862.   (Vol. 12, p. 583.)

DISCHARGE.

AN ACT to provide for granting an honorable discharge to coal-heavers
and firemen in the naval service.

Honorable discharges to firemen and coalheavers.
*Be it enacted by the Senate and House of Representatives of
the United States of America in Congress assembled*, That
honorable discharges may be granted to coal-heavers and
firemen in the naval service of the United States in the same
manner and subject to the same conditions as such discharges are now granted to seamen, ordinary seamen, landsmen and boys.*

Approved June 7, 1864.   (Vol. 13, p. 120.)

AN ACT to provide a more efficient discipline for the Navy.

Honorable discharges to seamen as a testimonial of fidelity and obedience.
Be it enacted &c., That from and after the passage of this
act, it shall be the duty of every commanding officer of any
of the vessels of the Navy, on returning from a cruise, to
forward, immediately on his arrival in port, to the Secretary
of the Navy, a list of the names of such of the crew† who
enlisted for three years, as, in his opinion, on being discharged, are entitled to an "honorable discharge," as a testimonial of fidelity and obedience; and that he shall grant
the same to such, according to the form to be prescribed by
the Secretary of the Navy.

Re-enlistments under an honorable discharge.
SEC. 2. *And be it further enacted*, That if any seaman, ordinary seaman, landsman, or boy, shall re-enlist for three
years, within three months after his discharge, he shall, on
presenting his honorable discharge, or on accounting in a
satisfactory manner for its loss, be entitled to pay during
the said three months, equal to that to which he would have
been entitled if he had been employed in actual service.

* * * * * *

Approved March 2, 1855.

---

* Portion of the act referred to above.

FUNERAL EXPENSES.

AN ACT making appropriations for the naval service for the year ending June thirtieth, eighteen hundred and seventy-one, and for other purposes.

SEC. 17. * * * Nor shall any funeral expenses of a naval officer who died in the United States, or expenses for travel to attend the funeral of an officer who died there, be allowed; but when an officer on duty dies in a foreign country, the expenses of his funeral, not exceeding his sea-pay for one month, shall be defrayed by the Government, and paid by the paymaster upon whose books the name of such officer was borne for pay.

No allowance for funeral expenses incurred in the United States.

In foreign countries one month's sea-pay allowed.

* * * * * *

Approved July 15, 1870.

List of engineers who have resigned from the Navy since the organization of the corps, August, 1842.

CHIEFS, 15.

Samuel Archbold,* March 18, 1861.	Robert H. Long, Oct. 31, 1863.
Alexander Birkbeck, Dec. 23, 1847.	Daniel B. Martin,* Nov. 22, 1859.
B. Edme Chassaing, Feb. 12, 1867.	William Roberts, March 18, 1869.
William E. Everett, Nov. 30, 1859.	William Sewell, Nov. 10, 1853.
John Faron, April 3, 1848.	Alban C. Stimers, Aug. 3, 1865.
Joshua Follansbee, May 1, 1865.	Charles B. Stuart,* June 30, 1853.
Jesse Gay, Oct. 22, 1859.	G. B. N. Tower, Sept. 29, 1865.
John A. Grier, Nov. 15, 1865	

* Engineer-in-chief.

FIRST ASSISTANTS, 60.

James M. Adams, Aug. 2, 1862.	Edward Mars, Feb. 11, 1862.
George W. Alexander, April 5, 1861.	Edward Marsland, June 4, 1864.
James Atkins, Aug. 1, 1865.	Henry Mason,* Nov. 14, 1853.
George J. Barry,* March 16, 1869.	John K. Matthews, May 17, 1849.
L. S. Bartholomew, April 20, 1847.	Samuel Matthews, July 18, 1849.
Emory J. Brooks, Dec. 7, 1868.	John M. Maury, Nov. 22, 1856.
Henry Brown, March 3, 1869.	Alexander McAusland, May 24, 1850.
S. Wilkins Cragg, April 11, 1870.	Henry C. McIlvaine, June 21, 1869.
Francis Cronin, Nov. 10, 1865.	Horace McMurtrie, Nov. 28, 1865.
Thomas S. Cunningham, Nov. 16, 1866.	William H. Messinger, June 16, 1865.
Nailor C. Davis, Oct. 29, 1859.	William J. Montgomery, Oct. 25, 1869.
Thomas M. Dukehart, March 9, 1871.	William Musgrave, Sept. 12, 1865.
E. A. C. Du Plaine, May 14, 1867.	Isaac Newton, Feb. 8, 1865.
Edward Faron, June 1, 1849.	William D. Pendleton, Jan. 4, 1866.
A. H. Fisher, Sept. 26, 1870.	James Renshaw, May 14, 1867.
Reuben H. Fitch, April 19, 1869.	William Roberts,* Aug. 24, 1859.
C. Wright Geddes, Sept. 5, 1855.	Henry W. Robie, May 25, 1868.
Levi R. Green, Aug. 2, 1869.	Hiram Sanford, Nov. 5, 1849.
David M. Greene, Sept. 16, 1869.	Samuel F. Savage, Jan. 13, 1865.
William K. Hall, Feb. 15, 1853.	William C. Selden, Oct. 19, 1868.
John T. Hawkins, Jan. 18, 1869.	Francis G. Smith, July 28, 1869.
William W. Hopper, Nov. 22, 1866.	Henry W. Spooner, May 23, 1859.
James B. Houston, July 28, 1865.	Robert S. Talbot, Oct. 24, 1868.
Jameson Cox Hull, Jan. 15, 1866.	Zephaniah Talbot, Dec. 16, 1865.
Thomas Kilpatrick, Aug. 22, 1853.	John D. Van Buren, Sept. 22, 1868.
Charlton B. Kid, Dec. 20, 1867.	Henry C. Victor, Dec. 16, 1863.
John L. Lay, May 22, 1865.	Philip R. Voorhees, Feb. 18, 1868.
Oscar C. Lewis, Sept. 28, 1868.	Edward A. Whipple, Feb. 20, 1854.
Orleans Longacre, June 6, 1866.	William C. Williamson, Jan. 10, 1866.
Francis J. Lovering, June 26, 1865.	James G. Young, Nov. 14, 1855.

* Reinstated.

SECOND ASSISTANTS, 146.

Francis B. Allen, Feb. 18, 1868.
Theodore Allen, June 13, 1865.
Oscar W. Allison, Dec. 8, 1869.
John H. Ames, Sept. 30, 1865.
Francis M. Ashton, Jan. 4, 1871.
William H. Badlam, March 10, 1866.
Charles H. Ball, Aug. 31, 1865.
William M. Barr, April 16, 1866.
George J. Barry,* Dec. 14, 1859.
Frederick W. Bissett, Oct. 22, 1867.
Edward S. Boynton, Nov. 7, 1863.
Theodore C. Brecht, Jan. 18, 1865.
E. Marshall Breese, March 2, 1868.
Jacob L. Bright, Oct. 18, 1870.
Amos Broadnix, Feb. 14, 1856.
Samuel R. Brooks, Dec. 13, 1865.
Nathan W. Buckhout, June 29, 1865.
Richard H. Buel, July 8, 1867.
Henry W. Bulkley, Oct. 14, 1865.
Benjamin Bunce, July 17, 1865.
Charles M. Burchard, July 26, 1865.
Harvey H. Burritt, Sept. 22, 1865.
Ten Eyck Byles, Oct. 25, 1858.
Albert B. Campbell, May 5, 1863.
Loudon Campbell, May 6, 1861.
Newton Champion, Sept. 22, 1863.
Edward Cheney, March 31, 1869.
William S. Cherry, Oct. 25, 1867.
Charles A. Chipley, April 9, 1862.
William J. Clark, Dec. 1, 1865.
Alfred Colin, Nov. 27, 1865.
Charles J. Coney, Oct. 2, 1866.
Gilbert C. Cook, July 22, 1865.
James G. Cooper, Dec. 19, 1865.
William H. Crawford, April 6, 1868.
John C. Cross, June 21, 1865.
Wayland Cuthbert, Aug. 22, 1864.
T. J. McK. Daniels, March 9, 1865.
Isaac De Graff, Aug. 23, 1866.
William H. De Hart, Nov. 5, 1869.
Herman A. Delins, June 22, 1865.
Richard D. Dodge, June 1, 1868.
William A. Dripps, Jan. 29, 1867.
Philip G. Eastwick, Aug. 5, 1865.
Robert N. Ellis, Oct. 15, 1867.
Charles E. Emery, Dec. 26, 1867.
John Everding, June 19, 1865.
James E. Fallon, May 21, 1866.
Henry Fauth, Aug. 29, 1856.
Frank H. Fletcher, Feb. 11, 1869.
Wilbur F. Fort, June 20, 1865.
John Franklin, June 26, 1865.
William Frick, jr., April 12, 1862.
Albert K. Fulton, April 25, 1864.
John Gallagher, Feb. 17, 1847.
Charles W. Geddes, Aug. 31, 1859.
Charles L. Greatrake, Oct. 25, 1847.
H. P. Gregory, April 27, 1865.
Levi Griffin, Nov. 2, 1847.
Thomas J. Griffin, April 6, 1863.
Franklin K. Haine, Jan. 24, 1863.
George W. Hall,* Nov. 16, 1866.
Alfred Hedrick, Aug. 9, 1865.
Edward L. Hewitt, Nov. 2, 1866.
James M. Hobby,* June 21, 1855.
Richard M. Hodgson, Dec. 21, 1868.
Charles F. Hollingsworth, Nov. 18, 1865.
Henry Holmes, Sept. 11, 1865.
George R. Holt, May 4, 1869.

Andrew P. How, Aug. 7, 1849.
Jameson C. Hull,* Sept. 22, 1856.
James W. Hutchinson, April 6, 1865.
John W. Huxley, June 16, 1865.
George C. Irelan, Nov. 10, 1865.
Albert Jackson, Sept. 23, 1865.
Owen Jones, Dec. 22, 1866.
James T. Kelcher, March 17, 1868.
William H. Kilpatrick, Feb. 9, 1866.
Glendy King, Sept. 7, 1858.
Myron H. Knapp, July 8, 1867.
Thomas La Blanc, Sept. 28, 1867.
Webster Lane, March 22, 1867.
Philip J. Langer, April 28, 1870.
William A. R. Latimer,* May 31, 1858.
William A. R. Latimer, Aug. 26, 1862.
John C. E. Lawrence, June 23, 1856.
E. D. Leavitt, May 25, 1867.
Edmund Lincoln, Feb. 4, 1863.
George D. Lining, April 18, 1861.
James Long, April 17, 1865.
Thomas Lynch, June 21, 1869.
Daniel T. Mapes, June 21, 1855.
Mason W. Mather, March 3, 1869.
James Maughlin, Aug. 11, 1865.
C. Stewart Maurice, Dec. 21, 1865.
William D. McIlvaine, Oct. 13, 1865.
S. Calvin McLanahan, June 21, 1869.
Hillary Messiner, Aug. 7, 1868.
Abram Michener, Sept. 25, 1865.
Frederick L. Miller, May 28, 1868.
William C. Monroe, March 1, 1871.
Joseph Morgan, Jan. 5, 1866.
Daniel Murphy, Nov. 25, 1848.
Munroe Murphy, Dec. 6, 1865.
John E. Neil, Nov. 23, 1865.
James J. Noble, March 3, 1866.
Isaac R. Oakford, Oct. 13, 1865.
Albert S. Palmer, July 15, 1848.
John W. Parkes, May 21, 1853.
Isaiah Paxon, Nov. 18, 1865.
James H. Perry, April 12, 1866.
Henry W. Phillips, July 28, 1869.
M. H. Plunkett, May 9, 1865.
William F. Pratt, July 29, 1865.
Franklin C. Prindle, Sept. 11, 1865.
Henry M. Quig, Nov. 26, 1869.
Richard B. Quin, Aug. 26, 1856.
Frederick T. H. Ramsden, April 14, 1869.
William J. Reid, Jan. 29, 1867.
George H. Riley, Oct. 17, 1865.
Edward E. Roberts, June 19, 1865.
George W. Rogers, June 23, 1865.
Augustine Sackett, Aug. 24, 1865.
Guy Samson, April 2, 1869.
George F. Sawyer, Oct. 12, 1868.
John K. Smedley, March 13, 1866.
Henry A. Smith, July 28, 1866.
Francis D. Stedman, Oct. 6, 1866.
Thomas A. Stephens, Sept. 6, 1853.
John C. Stevens, Oct. 25, 1866.
Charles H. Stone, June 10, 1865.
Lucien Sullivan, April 5, 1866.
Mark T. Sunstrom, Nov. 10, 1865.
Mosher A. Sutherland, Oct. 15, 1867.
William Taggert, May 12, 1849.
P. Henry Taylor, Sept. 10, 1856.
George W. Thorne, Nov. 5, 1863.
William W. Vanderbilt, Oct. 30, 1865.

* Reinstated.

Charles M. Van Tine, Jan. 4, 1866.
Edward D. Weems, Sept. 6, 1867.
Robert Weir, June 19, 1865.
William S. Wells, Oct. 12, 1870.
Philip H. White, April 27, 1865.

John Wilson, May 19, 1866.
Horace E. Winsor, Aug. 20, 1856.
James D. Wright, Oct. 16, 1861.
Robert A. Wright, Oct. 16, 1865.

THIRD ASSISTANTS, 125.

J. D. Alexander, Aug. 25, 1847.
Edward R. Archer, Nov. 3, 1860.
Edward R. Arnold, April 13, 1864.
LeRoy Arnold, Feb. 18, 1856.
George J. Barry,* Nov. 16, 1858.
James A. Barton, March 5, 1863.
Everett Battelle, July 25, 1864.
William S. Beau, Oct. 23, 1847.
Lemuel Bernard, March 21, 1866.
Peter C. Bogardus, Feb. 6, 1852.
William Bond, May 25, 1867.
Edward S. Boynton,* Oct. 15, 1860.
Charles D. Bray, March 18, 1869.
Frederick E. Brown, Oct. 24, 1859.
Samuel P. Budd, Aug. 10, 1867.
Lafayette Caldwell, June 12, 1849.
Francis A. Canfield, April 30, 1856.
George W. Carrick, Nov. 18, 1865.
Thomas Chase, Nov. 13, 1865.
Charles A. Chipley,* April 28, 1860.
Conrad J. Cooper, July 18, 1862.
John E. Cooper, May 14, 1863.
Robert A. Copeland, Aug. 1, 1859.
Sebastian Crolius, Aug. 13, 1862.
Thomas Crummey, Sept. 5, 1866.
Edward Curtis, Feb. 11, 1863.
Charles B. Dahlgren, Dec. 15, 1862.
Willis Davis, Nov. 4, 1850.
George E. De Luce, Feb. 28, 1853.
Jay Dinsmore, May 28, 1864.
George W. W. Dove, Aug. 10, 1863.
Frederick Eckel, Sept., 1863.
William R. Eckart, May 2, 1864.
Daniel B. Egbert, Jan. 21, 1865.
Clarence A. Evans, Sept. 4, 1865.
Wesley Fenimore, Oct. 12, 1865.
Samuel Fiske, June 12, 1858.
Cornelius A. Forbes, Nov. 5, 1847.
Joseph M. Freeman, Oct. 8, 1853.
William H. Fuller, Nov. 16, 1861.
George William Geddes, March 9, 1864.
F. A. R. George, Aug. 13, 1862.
Isaac I. Griffiths, Feb. 20, 1863.
Franklin K. Hain,* Aug. 9, 1858.
Hiram Haines, July 25, 1854.
Francis P. Hallowell, Nov. 12, 1867.
Richard E. Halsey, Oct. 30, 1863.
Robert F. Hatfield, July 18, 1862.
Henry D. Heiser, April 22, 1865.
George P. Houston, Jan. 28, 1860.
John Howell, May 3, 1856.
Charles Sedgwick Hunt, June 9, 1863.
Henry C. Jewell, Jan. 11, 1854.
Benjamin Kavanaugh,* Dec. 21, 1861.
Henry H. Kimball, June 29, 1869.
Ingersoll F. Knowlton, March 17, 1865.
Lewis C. F. Laesch, May 24, 1864.
Henry R. Lawrence,* Nov. 9, 1861.
Henry R. Lawrence, March 21, 1863.
Nelson H. Lawton, April 25, 1865.
Columbus W. Lee, June 2, 1855.
James D. Lee, Nov. 10, 1866.
J. Henry Lewars, June 29, 1868.

Cleland Lindsley, Aug. 30, 1856.
John H. Long,* Nov. 5, 1850.
Henry F. Loveaire, Oct. 26, 1868.
William Luce, May 29, 1847.
George W. Magee,* April 7, 1863.
Charles H. Manson, Nov. 25, 1853.
Charles F. Marsland, Sept. 6, 1865.
Henry McConnell, Feb. 6, 1868.
Samuel McElroy, July 20, 1852.
Sylvanus McIntyre, June 19, 1865.
John E. McKay, July 7, 1860.
John D. Mercer, July 8, 1856.
Joseph Mercer, May 1, 1852.
William W. Miller, Aug. 5, 1851.
Augustus Mitchell,* May 1, 1862.
John C. Mitchell,* April 28, 1853.
John C. Mitchell, Nov. 16, 1854.
T. M. Mitchell, Dec. 6, 1862.
Cyrus R. Morgan, April 2, 1864.
Charles R. Mosher, March 3, 1866.
Jacob M. Murray, May 13, 1865.
Augustus F. Nagle, May 3, 1865.
Henry B Nones,* Aug. 19, 1856.
Frank W. Nyman, April 21, 1864.
L. L. Olmsted, Sept. 22, 1862.
Cornelius T. Parke, May 31, 1854.
George Paul, Sept. 9, 1865.
John B. Peck, June 7, 1869.
Gustavus A. Pfeltz, June 25, 1866.
William L. Phillips, July 6, 1860.
Granville Toucey Pierce, Aug. 8, 1857.
Boaz E. Pike, April 6, 1864.
John L. Plumly, Aug. 29, 1860.
James Plunkett, Feb. 6, 1861.
G. M. Plympton, Dec. 19, 1854.
William A. Powers, March 3, 1866.
Erastus P. Rank, March 9, 1865.
W. C. F. Reichenbach, Nov. 27, 1866.
Peter C. Reilly, Oct. 20, 1863.
Z. K. Rind, Nov. 10, 1858.
Alexander H. Roane, Feb. 11, 1850.
William W. Shipman, Feb. 27, 1862.
Samuel O. Shorey, June 3, 1854.
Theron Skeel, Nov. 12, 1870.
Thaddeus S. Smith, July 8, 1862.
William C. Starr, May 28, 1862.
Robert S. Stedman, April 5, 1865.
John Stell, Sept. 18, 1863.
George W. Tennent, Feb. 6, 1861.
M. M. Thompson, Aug. 25, 1847.
Smith Thompson, Jan. 13, 1846.
James H. Toombs, April 24, 1861.
Frank H. Townsend, April 12, 1866.
Francis N. Trevor, June 26, 1869.
James Wallace, Aug. 8, 1859.
Jesse F. Walton, March 31, 1865.
Robert L. Wamaling, Nov. 17, 1865.
Charles K. Warner, Oct. 11, 1866.
Joseph H. Warrington, Feb. 1, 1860.
George H. White, Oct. 14, 1859.
G. W. Wilkinson, Sept. 22, 1863.
William W. Willett, March 6, 1857.
George R. Woodend, April 20, 1857.

* Reinstated.

Engineers who have died in the service.

CHIEFS, 12.

William H. Cushman, November 2, 1865, Philadelphia, Pennsylvania.
John Faron, August 5, 1864, lost on the Tecumseh, Mobile Bay.
George Gideon, June 16, 1863, Philadelphia, Pennsylvania.
Alexander Greer, September 10, 1867, on board the Tuscarora, South Pacific.
Andrew Hebard, August 4, 1846, Buffalo, New York.
Eben Hoyt, October 19, 1867, killed by bursting of boiler of steam-launch at the Naval Academy, Annapolis, Maryland.
Henry Hunt, April 10, 1861, Philadelphia, Pennsylvania.
Mortimer Kellogg, November 16, 1870, Key West, Florida.
Andrew Lawton, March 17, 1871, Philadelphia, Pennsylvania.
Robert W. McLeery, September 15, 1863, Philadelphia, Pennsylvania.
Philip G. Peltz, August 21, 1868, on the Pacific coast.
John P. Whipple, September 26, 1864, Key West, Florida.

FIRST ASSISTANTS, 16.

John Alexander, January 26, 1863, Baltimore, Maryland.
Haviland Barstow, January 24, 1870, lost on board the Oneida, Yokohama Bay, Japan.
Thomas H. Bordley, December 10, 1865, Bahia, South America.
Joseph N. Cahill, April 15, 1864, killed by the boiler explosion on board the Chenango.
E. G. Covell, December 28, 1847, off Tuspan, of fever.
James W. De Krafft, October 19, 1870, Washington, District of Columbia.
Reynolds Driver, October 2, 1866, New Castle, Delaware.
William Holland, August 18, 1856, Newark, Delaware.
John H. Hunt, November 21, 1868, Mare Island, California.
William H. King, April 25, 1859, Warrington, Florida.
Nicholas B. Littig, January 24, 1870, lost on board the Oneida, Yokohama Bay, Japan.
Henry H. Molony, October, 1865, lost on board the Atlanta.
Jesse Rutherford, January 3, 1862, Philadelphia, Pennsylvania.
Edward Scattergood, September 20, 1864, on board the Maratanza.
Henry W. Scott, May 10, 1869, Flushing, Long Island.
Joseph Watters, September 13, 1866, New Orleans, Louisiana.

SECOND ASSISTANTS, 33.

Frederick S. Barlow, August 5, 1864, lost on board the Tecumseh, Mobile Bay.
George F. Barton, September 4, 1853, naval hospital, Pensacola, Florida.
Andrew Blythe, April 19, 1870, New York.
Jared H. Botsford, July 25, 1864, hospital ship Falcon, New York.
Alfred S. Brower, January 17, 1867, Brooklyn, New York.
Frederick E. Brown, December 12, 1864, New York.
Frederick Bull, jr., August 9, 1863, on board the Pocahontas, off New Orleans, Louisiana.
Joel A. Bullard, March 22, 1866, on board the Kearsarge, at sea, of yellow fever.
Joseph L. Butler, September 14, 1862.
Thomas Cronin, December 8, 1861, Philadelphia, Pennsylvania.
Eli Crosby, January 24, 1854, on board the Susquehanna, Napa Roads, East Indies.
Oscar Davids, February 9, 1859, Norfolk, Virginia.
Theodore Ely.
Morgan H. English, December 23, 1862, Washington, District of Columbia.
John Fornance, January 24, 1870, lost on board the Oneida, Yokohama Bay, Japan.
Edward Gay, January 19, 1870, Green Point, Long Island.
James M. Harris, October 6, 1864, Pensacola, Florida.
Elisha Harsen, August 5, 1864, lost on board the Tecumseh, Mobile Bay.
Jackson R. Hatcher, December 23, 1858, Norfolk, Virginia.
John Hollins, June 4, 1858, at sea.
Joseph Hoops, March 18, 1866, on board the Kearsarge, at sea, of yellow fever.
Samuel H. Houston, June 16, 1854, Navy hospital, Brooklyn, New York.
Simon B. Knox, September 19, 1855, Warrington, Florida.
Henry S. Leonard, August 5, 1864, lost on board the Tecumseh, Mobile Bay.
John McIntyre, May 21, 1865, Philadelphia, Pennsylvania.
James B. McNamara, June 23, 1864, on board the Tioga, at sea.

Albert S. Murray, April 15, 1864, killed by explosion of the boiler on board the Chenanga, New York Bay.

Washington H. Nones, September 9, 1853, naval hospital, Pensacola, Florida, of yellow fever.

Charles W. C. Senter, January 24, 1870, lost on board the Oneida, Yokohama Bay, Japan.

Thomas A. Stephens, August, 1864, Philadelphia, Pennsylvania.

Joseph W. Sydney, October 31, 1864, on board the Pembina, off Brazos, Texas.

Robert L. Webb, June 13, 1870, Tulcahuano, Chili.

James Wylie, April 26, 1869, at the British hospital, Callao, Peru, of yellow fever.

THIRD ASSISTANTS, 35.

George A. Baker, June 6, 1864, naval hospital, Portsmouth, Virginia.

Henry S. Barker, July 25, 1855, Buffalo, New York.

Patrick Henry Barry, August 1, 1863, Eastport, Maine.

James M. Benckert, June 28, 1862, on board the Itasca.

Joseph Bilisoly, September 3, 1855, Portsmouth, Virginia, of yellow fever.

John Carroll, December 21, 1851, on board the Warren, San Francisco, California.

Edward W. Clark, July 1, 1866, Philadelphia, Pennsylvania.

Dewitt G. Davis, January 15, 1865, lost on board the Patapsco, Charleston Harbor.

Thomas Dickson, September 12, 1847, Norfolk hospital, Virginia.

Frederick Dobbs, April 29, 1862, Williamsburgh, New York.

Richard F. Edwards, March 23, 1866, on board the Kearsarge, at sea, of yellow fever.

Isaac B. Fort, December 1, 1865, Washington, District of Columbia.

William H. Gamble, August 26, 1862, Pensacola, Florida, of yellow fever.

William T. Gorton, August 31, 1853, Pensacola hospital, of yellow fever.

Robinson W. Hands, December 31, 1862, lost in the Monitor, off Hatteras.

Lewis A. Haverly, August 29, 1862, naval hospital, Norfolk, Virginia.

John C. Huntly, October 20, 1863, New Orleans, Louisiana, of yellow fever.

Samuel C. Latimer, August 24, 1855, from the effects of the bursting of the Hetzel's boiler.

William Francis Law, September 24, 1863, naval hospital, New Orleans, Louisiana, of yellow fever.

Samuel A. Lewis, December 31, 1862, lost in the Monitor, off Hatteras.

Charles A. Mapes, November 12, 1847, on board the Mississippi, at Sacrificios, of fever.

James McGregor, September 22, 1863, naval hospital, New Orleans, Louisiana.

Henry W. Merian, December 6, 1863, lost in the Weehawken, off Charleston.

Augustus Mitchell, December 6, 1863, lost in the Weehawken, off Charleston.

William D. Park, July 11, 1863, on board the Richmond, in the Mississippi River.

Peter A. Sassé.

William R. Schley, February 25, 1858, Valparaiso, Chili.

Charles P. Scott, June 20, 1864, on board the Tioga.

E. H. Seymour, April 11, 1864, Middlebury, Vermont.

George E. Shock, September 11, 1853, East Pascagoula, Mississippi, of yellow fever.

Benjamin R. Stevens, June 15, 1865, lost on the Patapsco, Charleston Harbor.

Elijah R. Tyson, March 23, 1866, on board the Kearsarge, at sea, of yellow fever.

I. A. Van Zandt, April 7, 1849, Washington, District of Columbia.

William L. Walters, May 27, 1858, on board the Merrimack, at Panama.

John M. Whittemore, November 7, 1861, in action off Hilton Head, South Carolina.

Engineers who have left the service otherwise than as above specified.

CHIEFS, 9.

Charles H. Haswell,* Dec. 1, 1850.	Michael Quinn, May 18, 1861.
Thomas A. Jackson, May 6, 1861.	James H. Warner, July 8, 1861.
James F. Lamden, March 5, 1867.	William C. Wheeler, Jan. 17, 1863.
Charles B. Moss, Jan. 30, 1846.	William P. Williamson, May 6, 1861.
Nathanial P. Patterson, June 10, 1861.	

* Engineer-in-chief.

5 E C

First Assistants, 10.

George W. City, Aug. 1, 1861.
William P. De Sanno, March 19, 1862.
Virginius Freeman, July 8, 1861.
George F. Hebard, Sep. 17, 1856.
Edward W. Manning, May 6, 1861.

Philip L. Mars, Nov. 2, 1861.
Richard C. Potts, June 15, 1861.
Henry A. Ramsay, May 6, 1861.
Charles Schroeder, May 18, 1861.
T. B. C. Stump, May 22, 1861.

Second Assistants, 21.

James Atkinson, Jan. 18, 1848.
Alexander Auchinleck, July 28, 1848.
Benjamin D. Clemens, Jan. 12, 1866.
Robert A. Copeland, Sept. 19, 1861.
S. Wilkins Cragg,* June 27, 1864.
Frank H. Fletcher, Feb. 11, 1869.
Charles W. Geddes, Aug. 31, 1859.
Marshal P. Jordan, May 20, 1861.
William H. Kelly, Nov. 20, 1866.
Glendy King, June 13, 1861.
Edward W. Koehl, Jan. 9, 1867.

Elijah Laws,* May 27, 1863.
Charles W. Levy, July 6, 1861.
George T. W. Logan, Aug. 29, 1856.
William T. Mercier, Aug. 14, 1849.
John M. Middleton, Oct. 5, 1849.
William Pollard,* Oct. 18, 1867.
William Scott, June 5, 1850.
F. A. Shuck, Aug. 7, 1847.
John C. Tennent, July 5, 1849.
John W. Tynan, May 6, 1861.

Third Assistants, 40.

Edward R. Arnold, April 13, 1864.
A. G. Bonsall, Jan. 12, 1866.
Walter Pearce Burrow, May 17, 1860.
Charles Coleman, Dec. 15, 1851.
Charles C. Davis, Dec. 30, 1863.
John C. Denby, Sept. 1, 1864.
Edward L. Dick, May 28, 1861.
William Dunham, April 8, 1847.
Albert C. Engard,* Aug. 6, 1866.
Henry Fagan, July 8, 1861.
William H. Glading, Aug. 4, 1863.
John P. Green, March 1, 1862.
Richard D. Guerard, July 20, 1850.
William M. Habirshaw, Feb. 5, 1862.
Thomas J. Harris, July 7, 1849.
Andrew H. Henderson, April 17, 1866.
Benjamin Herring, July 8, 1861.
Edward S. Hutchinson, Jan. 21, 1862.
Edward C. Johnson.
Charles W. Jordan, May 6, 1861.

S. Cushing Lane, April 8, 1865.
William F. Lynch, Feb. 5, 1852.
Gates McAllister, March 18, 1867.
B. J. McGurren, Oct. 28, 1863.
Noah W. Moffett, Sep. 16, 1863.
Charles F. Nagle,* Jan. 8, 1866.
William Dunlap Park, Feb. 17, 1862.
Edwin C. Patten, Jan. 8, 1861.
Thomas Petherick, Nov. 26, 1862.
William Pollard,* Jan. 24, 1862.
Joseph R. Pomroy, Dec. 20, 1852.
John Serra, Feb. 27, 1851.
James E. Speights, March 21, 1868.
John K. Stevenson, Aug. 2, 1869.
Frederick G. Sumwalt, Sept. 29, 1854.
George F. Sweet, Jan. 30, 1869.
Henry T. Tapman, Sept. 13, 1864.
Winfield S. Thompson.
John T. Tucker, May 6, 1861.
Henry X. Wright, May 6, 1861.

* Reappointed.

INDEX.